# Wishing Upon a Star

## CHRISTINA BERRY

**Copyright © 2022 by Christina Berry**

All rights reserved.

This is a work of fiction. Names, characters, places, and incidents are the products of the author's imagination or used fictitiously. Any resemblance to actual events, places, or persons, living or dead, is purely coincidental.

No portion of this book may be reproduced in any form or by any electric or mechanical means, including information or retrieval systems, without prior written permission from the publisher.

**Published by PVR Publishing**

Edited by VB Edits

Cover illustration by Novinkina Xeniya

Cover formatting by Sarah Kil Creative Studio

*For Spike*

# CHAPTER 1
*Scarlet*

"Wasn't it John Ritter's character, Ted Buchanan?" Julie ponders.

"No. It was Malcolm in season one," I say.

"He wasn't a robot," Paula argues. "He was a demon who got loose on the internet and catfished Willow."

"The name of the episode is literally, 'I, Robot… You, Jane,' and he embodied a mechanical form so he could become corporeal. Trust me, he's a robot. Everyone else will guess Ted, but we'll get it right by choosing Malcolm." I shrug. "If the answer is Ted, then the trivia question is flawed."

Julie nods as she writes down our answer.

Gayle Weathers, tonight's quizmaster, repeats the question, her radio-smooth voice booming through the microphone and bouncing from the peak of the wooden ceiling overhead. "Name the first character on *Buffy* who was a robot."

"This is too easy," Paula says and chugs her beer.

"Only because we have the Buffy Bot on our team." Julie nods toward me and elbows Paula in the stomach. Paula nearly spits beer all over the table and those of us around it.

I smirk at Julie for the weird nickname, though she's not entirely wrong. I'm probably the second biggest *Buffy the Vampire Slayer* nerd in the Tahoe region—Gayle, our quizmaster and part owner of the Silver Lining bar, takes top spot, which is how *I* know that *she* knows the correct answer to her question.

Finishing the last sip of my drink, I settle deeper into my seat, finally relaxing after an hours-long management meeting in San Jose and my last-minute flight to make it in time for the *Buffy* version of TNT (Tuesday Night Trivia) here at The Silver Lining.

"I'm getting nachos and another beer. Anyone want anything?" Paula asks as she stands and brushes the creases from her skirt.

"Mmm, nachos." Julie licks her lips.

I wave my empty tumbler of rum and Coke at her, and Paula heads to the bar. I turn back to Julie, who's clearly been wanting to get me alone all night.

"I think he's going to ask her." She bounces in her seat.

"Who's asking whom what?"

Julie frowns. "Steve is going to ask Paula to marry him."

"Oh." I don't know how to feel about the news. They've been together since high school, and we graduated almost ten years ago. How long does it take a guy to figure out a woman is his forever person? Either Steve is really slow, or he thinks he's settling for Paula, which pisses me off because she's amazing, and he's lucky to have her. "Cool."

"Cool? Really? That's your response?"

"Did you want me to squeal like an otter and do cartwheels across the bar?"

"Just...be happy for her. Please?" Julie pleads. "She doesn't need another anti-man earful from you. Let her have this, okay?"

"Anti-man?" I'm stunned. "What do you mean?"

"Oh please. To you, men are just dicks with legs attached so they can move those dicks from woman to woman."

"Well, yeah, but…I like their dicks; that's my favorite part of them. I'm not anti-man."

"Okay, so then you're anti-relationship," Julie settles.

"I am not—"

"When was the last time you dated someone for more than a week?"

*Just because I have more important things to do than date, doesn't mean I'm anti-man or anti-relationship.*

"And when, miracle of miracles, you do date, you break up with them for the weirdest reasons."

"I do not."

"Remember Evan? You broke up with him because he put emojis in a text."

"We were supposed to meet at his office for lunch, and when I asked what he wanted, he replied with an eggplant, a tongue, and that water droplet emoji."

"Subtle." Julie smirks.

"Juvenile. He's supposedly the best real estate lawyer in the Bay Area and he can't use his words to ask for a blowjob?"

Julie howls with laughter. "If he had used his words like a big boy, would you have given him a lunch-time blowjob?"

I shrug. *Probably.*

"You know what you need?" *I need this conversation to end.* "You need to fall in love. That'll change everything for you. When you're in love, your man can send you all the eggplant emojis he wants, and you'll let him because you'll think it's cute."

"That sounds awful," I grumble.

"Says the woman who's never been in love."

That's not true. I was in love once. It was unrequited and it sucked.

These days, I'm too busy for any attempt at a real relationship. Besides, who am I going to date? I'll skip the mile-long line of morons who want to brag about banging a billionaire. Miss me with the beautiful boys who want to be kept by the youngest sugar mama in recorded history, too.

When the itch twitches, I find someone to scratch it, sure. But I keep my dates practical and efficient—friendship and sex without the time-consuming complication of a relationship. I get what I want, they get what they want—eggplant emojis aside—and we go on our merry ways.

Julie is a diehard romantic. It doesn't matter how many times her heart has been broken; she always puts it back out there. It's once bitten twice shy for me. She can have her romances, and I'll keep my flings.

"Oh my God, you'll never guess who's here," Paula says when she returns to the table with her beer and my cocktail, then she walks away.

We frown at her back as she returns to the bar to collect our nachos. I scan the room, curious about who this mystery person might be.

And that's when I see him.

He's impossible to miss. He always was.

Hair so black it's almost blue, soft midnight waves that curl enticingly at the collar of his shirt. I remember following him toward the cafeteria after chem class, watching the way the florescent lights of the stairwell would shine like a halo on those dark tresses. His eyes are iceberg-aqua blue, the perfect color. I chose tile in that exact shade to line my pool. Not for any particular reason, of course.

It's his mouth, though, that I can't take my eyes off. There was a time when I would have given anything to know the taste of that mouth, the feel of it.

"Griffin Stone!" Paula confirms as she sets the heaping pile of nachos on the table between us.

"No way!" Julie perks up, scanning the crowd for a glimpse.

The urge to slide down in my seat like a boneless puddle of goo and hide beneath the high-top table hits me, just like in high school. Jesus, one look at the guy and I've morphed back into the spineless little wall flower I used to be.

"Didn't you tutor him, Scarlet? What was he like?"

*An enigma: at times the sweetest guy on Earth, and at other times an entitled asshole who delighted in tormenting me.* "He was all right," I say with a shrug, like it was all meaningless. Like Griffin Stone wasn't the first and only love of my life. Like his practical jokes didn't repeatedly break my heart. Like his kindnesses weren't the only things that could mend it. I add, "His dad paid me a hundred dollars a week to make sure he passed math. I bought Beulah with that money."

"Beulah!" They laugh at the memory of my vintage VW Bug, the car we tootled around town in that last summer before I drove her all the way to MIT in the fall, ready to start my new life.

"All right, everyone, ready to start the next round? For this section we'll be playing name that band." Quizmaster Gayle's voice is a soothing balm, allowing me to forget all about Griffin fucking Stone.

The *Buffy the Vampire Slayer* opening credit music plays and we say, "Nerf Herder," in unison as we stuff nachos into our mouths and Julie writes down our answer.

# CHAPTER 2
## *Griffin*

I bob my head to the opening music from *Buffy the Vampire Slayer*, and it reminds me of Scarlet Branson. She'd been a big *Buffy* fan.

*Damn, I haven't thought about her in ages.*

Scarlet—the perfect name for the girl with long curly red hair and heart-breaker green eyes—will forever be the one that got away. I'd crushed on her as far back as English class in tenth grade. She sat in front of me, and I spent the hour leaning in close, smelling the strawberry scent of her hair. I'd never paid more attention in a class. I was always trying to impress Scarlet by knowing the answers to the teacher's questions or having an opinion about Iago's treatment of Desdemona and Candide's blind optimism.

I wanted Scarlet to think I was smart like her. But any illusion of intelligence was dashed when my asshole father hired her to tutor me in math. As much as I'd savored my time with her during our senior year, I'd hated it, too.

I became familiar with the sound of her laughter, since that was her reaction every time I invited her to a game to watch me play. And worse than that was the time she rolled her eyes—who does that?—when I asked her to prom.

Scarlet was the one girl I truly wanted, and she was the only girl who wouldn't give me the time of day—beyond the time my father paid her for. It was a crushing lesson in humility for me, Mr. Most Likely to Succeed.

But that was then. And this is now. I have succeeded, phenomenally. That old wound can't hurt me anymore.

I stretch across the pool table, lining up my shot while the other half of the bar titters with conversation and *Buffy* music. I shoot and miss when I jerk my stick at the sudden noise as Gayle Weathers, the trivia announcer, starts a new song.

I frown at Rob. "What have you brought me into, man? Ladies' Night at The Silver Lining?"

As if on cue, a woman winks at me as she shimmies past us toward the bar.

"I forgot about Tuesday Night Trivia." Rob shrugs, lining up his own shot and making it. "Besides, isn't this, like, your demographic? The teen paranormal drama types?"

I smirk at him, a little annoyed but mostly amused. He's not wrong. I've starred as the main character on the paranormal detective show *White Knightshade* for seven seasons. Of course, that's all over now. I haven't told Rob, or anyone, the big news. I'm expressly forbidden from sharing the details by the terms of my nondisclosure agreement. After all, it would be a major spoiler if the star of the show told the world his character was going to be killed in the upcoming season finale.

Three weeks—three remaining episodes—before the world learns I'm unemployed. At least the death scene was pretty epic. A vampire torn apart by werewolves as the sun rises on the day of a full moon? Very cinematic.

"How long are you in town for this time?"

I shrug, hoping he gets the *I don't know and don't care* vibe I'm doing my best to fake. You'd think I'd be a better actor by now, but Rob raises a brow when I say, "Until they call me back."

Truth is, I don't want to go back at all. I'd like to avoid the paparazzi frenzy when news of Darius Nightshade's demise hits the streets. Plus, I'm avoiding my agent. He's been crawling up my ass to accept a role in an indie film where I play a serial rapist.

*"You need a departure from the Darius character, or you risk being typecast,"* Anson says to my voice mail twice daily. From a vampire detective to a serial rapist? Can't he find me a role in a rom-com? I could play the grumpy single dad of a precocious child who falls in love with the woman next door. That would be a departure. And a lot less, you know, rapey.

Maybe it's cowardly to come home and hide out. But here I am, playing pool with my best friend from high school while The Sundays' version of "Wild Horses" plays. I remember that scene from *Buffy*—I watched every episode of the show so I'd have something to talk to Scarlet about between her explanation of equations. This song was from Buffy's prom. She'd invited Angel, and he'd said no, but he showed up anyway, and they slow danced to "Wild Horses."

I'd stupidly gone to our prom alone, too. I'd invited Scarlet, and she'd rolled her eyes in reply. Still, I naively hoped for that romantic moment when she'd show up anyway, like an Angel-surprise. She didn't.

I was such a sap; a hopeless romantic. Scarlet bruised that part of me, but Hollywood quickly crushed it completely. Looking back, I'm embarrassed by how desperate I was for her attention.

"Oh shit," Rob says and laughs as he goes on, "don't look now, but isn't that the brainy chick you were always mooning over in high school?"

*Oh Jesus. No way.*

I glance to where Rob nods his head and instantly spot Scarlet's scarlet-red hair. She's exactly how I remember her, only more beautiful now. The last ten years have been kind, very kind.

I realize I'm staring when Rob elbows me in the ribs. "You should go say hi, big shot. You're Mr. Hollywood now; she has to say yes to you."

"No one *has* to say yes to anyone for anything," I scoff. I'm probably overly sensitive since my agent wants to cast me as a rapist.

"It was a joke," Rob grumbles.

"Not a good one."

"With ninety-nine points, tonight's winning team is," Gayle pauses for dramatic effect, "the Scooby Snacks!"

Scarlet and her friends—both of whom I recognize from high school—hug and high five. I nearly drop my pool stick when, mid-celebration, Scarlet looks across the room and zeros in on me. Caught staring, I raise a hand in a half-assed wave at her. She half-ass waves back, then she pulls away from her friend, tucks a strand of that gorgeous red hair behind her ear, and turns her attention back to the nachos.

# CHAPTER 3
*Scarlet*

"I invited them over," Julie stage whispers as she slides back onto her chair.

"You did what?" I shout, and both ladies hush me as Rob and Griffin join us. I vaguely remember Rob. He was on the baseball team with Griffin and went into the minor leagues after graduation. But none of that matters to me as my focus darts to Griffin. He's standing beside Rob with a smooth grin on his face and a half-empty bottle of beer in his hand.

His teeth are straighter and whiter than before, his complexion is clearer, and he's grown into his ears, which were big for his face when we were kids. His shoulders are wider now, and the way his shirt clings to his muscles is distracting.

"Hi," Julie and Paula say brightly to the two men.

Somehow Griffin ends up beside me. I scooch my stool over to make more room for him, and he scooches, too, until I'm wedged against Julie's side. He's so close I feel the heat from his body all over mine.

"Hi," Rob and Griffin respond to Julie and Paula. Then things get awkward. I expect someone to say something; perhaps Julie could quiz Griffin about his television career or ask Rob how the minor leagues are treating him. Instead, they all stare at me as if waiting for me to speak.

*What?*

*Oh. Right.*

"Hi," I add, giving another stupid wave like the one I sent Griffin when he caught me looking at him.

Griffin grins from half his mouth like he used to. God, that expression can still melt me from the inside out.

I cool down with a guzzle of my rum and Coke before I remember that I have to boat home. I grab the glass of water Paula brought me a while ago and chug most of it.

It's strange to be so close to Griffin again. His proximity brings out the worst in me, like it always did. In a matter of seconds, I'm transformed from a capable, independent woman to a nervous little girl staring at my lap.

It pisses me off. I'm better than this. I am no longer that stupid girl who laughed along every time Griffin amused himself by asking me on a date. I always wondered what would've happened if I'd said yes to him. Would it have been a bucket of pig's blood and psychic slaughter at the prom, a la *Carrie*? Or would I have found out later he'd lost a bet with his friends and was forced to be seen in public with "Scabby Scar"?

Jeez, I got scratched up in one bicycle accident in the seventh grade and was stuck with that horrible nickname for the entirety of my adolescence. Kids are so cruel.

But I'm not a kid anymore. I will not be ruled by these childish emotions and insecurities. I'm Scarlet fucking Branson. I make grown men quake in their loafers when they step into my office. I may not have been in Griffin Stone's league back then, but I'm well above it now.

I raise my head in defiance and give Griffin my most professional smile as Julie takes over the conversation. "I watch your show every week."

Everyone nods. They all watch his show. I do, too. Teen

paranormal melodrama is my kryptonite. From *Buffy the Vampire Slayer* to *The Vampire Diaries* to *Teen Wolf* to *White Knightshade*, I'm hooked. Doesn't hurt that Griffin looks gorgeous in fangs, but I'm not about to admit that to him.

Paula peppers him with questions: "Is it Lucian's or Darius's baby Belladonna is carrying? Did the werewolf bite Valentina, or was it a scratch? Is she going to turn? And what was up with that ghost guy at the end of the last episode?"

"I can't say a word." Griffin gives her a too-perfect grin; he's performing for her.

"Oh come on, you can trust us. Just one little spoiler?" Julie joins in.

Everyone at the table leans in like we're going to swap secrets. It's too much. Griffin is too close and he smells too good. I need to get out of here, but he's blocking my exit.

"Would you excuse me?" I give Griffin my own fake grin.

He shifts aside, and I aim for the bar and the handsome man serving drinks. "May I have a water, please?"

Freed from the confines of the table, I take a big whiff of air which smells too much like stale beer, perfume, and... Griffin?

*Oh no. Did he follow me over—?*

"I'll have what she's having, and the drinks are on me," Griffin says as he leans beside me.

The bartender frowns at him as he slides my water across the bar. "You got it, big spender. Another water coming right up."

I can't help but laugh.

Griffin smirks as he stuffs a twenty in the tip jar and puts his wallet back in his pants. "I always could make you laugh at me, Scar."

I stop laughing. "I hate that nickname."

Griffin grabs his glass and winks at me over the rim when he says, "I know."

I frown at him as I sip my water, unable to fathom why, if

he knew I hated it, he repeatedly used it. Or why he's winking at me now like we're sharing some cute inside joke.

He cracks that cocky half grin, the one I've always loved and hated in equal measure, and asks, "How long has it been?"

"Ten years," I answer.

He shakes his head. "You look amazing. Not a day over twenty-two."

Leave it to the Hollywood heartthrob with glowing teeth to assume I covet youth. In my field, youth is a challenge I've had to overcome to be taken seriously. I've worked my ass off to prove I'm not some dumb little girl wanting to play with the big boys.

"What have you been up to since high school?" he asks, awkwardly moving from one foot to the other, and I realize how little I've spoken.

"Graduated from college—"

"MIT, right?"

I nod.

"Impressive."

"Went to work in Silicon Valley. Doing well."

"That's great."

"I'd ask what you've been up to since high school, but everyone already knows: the great Griffin Stone, starring as Darius Nightshade, the night-crawling vampire leader of the White Knightshade Paranormal Detective Agency on the highest-rated paranormal teen detective melodrama in cable history. Very impressive."

"It's a living." He grimaces and changes the subject. "So what are you doing in Tahoe on a Tuesday?"

"I live here. Well, part time. I bought a house on the lake."

"Oh yeah? Where?"

"Rubicon Bay."

"Lakefront? Impressive. Who'd you have to divorce to afford that?"

I choke on my water, because *is he serious*? Who *the fuck* does he think he is?

Griffin backpedals. "I'm sorry. That was a very bad joke and presumptuous of me. Are you married? I noticed you aren't wearing a ring, so I…"

I stop listening. It doesn't matter what he has to say now. For as long as I've known this man, I've let him tangle me in knots. My heart still pitter patters at the sight of him, and his so-called humor still has the power to poke holes in my self-esteem.

But no more. I will not allow Griffin Stone to revert me to a socially awkward, heartbroken teenager crushing on the boy who never saw me and clearly never will.

With every ounce of steel I can forge into my spine, I hold my head high and interrupt his inept apology with a curt farewell. "It was nice catching up, Griffin, but I'm going to go."

Then I leave.

## CHAPTER 4
*Griffin*

What just happened? We were talking like old friends, and then bam, she leaves. She leveled those moody green eyes at me, set the water I "bought" her down, and walked right out the door.

No one could ever bring me down a peg like Scarlet. Those network producers who told me I was aging out of teen drama and had to be killed in a gory werewolf orgy could stand to take castration lessons from her. None of those pricks could cut me down to size *and* make me enjoy it like Scarlet does. So, because I must be a masochist, I follow her.

I stomp out the back door of the bar, surprised to find her walking in the direction of the pier, not the parking lot. She has her heels in her hands as she navigates the sand and hops onto the dock, unlocking the gate and aiming for a nice bowrider boat tied to the end.

The gate closes before I reach it, and I'm locked out, so I holler. "Scar, what the hell? Why are you leaving?"

She spins on her heels and storms back toward me, the dock undulating with the angry sway of her hips. "For the love of God, Griffin, stop calling me Scar!"

I like the way her cheeks pinken when she gets all riled up. "Ah, lighten up. It's just a joke."

"Of course it's just a joke. Everything you say is 'just a joke,' even when it's not funny. Even when it's rude and hurtful. You haven't changed a bit, have you?"

That stings. "Rude and hurtful? What are you talking about? Scar is a badass nickname."

"A scar is a wound. Maybe that'd be a badass nickname for a tough guy who survived a knife fight, but it's not a 'badass' nickname for a shy sixteen-year-old girl forced to tutor her childhood crush."

*Wait. What?*

Like she's realized too late what she said, she shakes her head, then turns back to her boat. Without a backward glance, she unties it from the dock, slips on a life vest, and throttles away.

I'm frozen stiff, unable to move. *Did she call me her childhood crush?*

~

Back inside, I go to the table where Rob leans into the hot blonde. She—I think her name is Julie—scowls at me. "Did she leave?"

"Yes."

"Why? What did you say?"

"Nothing."

"You had to say something. Scarlet doesn't scare easily."

"She was mad because I called her Scar."

The brunette, Paula, I think, asks, "And?"

I shrug and slump into Scarlet's empty chair. "I don't know. We were talking about where she lives, and I made a joke about her being divorced."

"She's not divorced."

"It was a dumb joke."

"What joke?"

Rob watches the volley between Julie and me like he's at a tennis match, and I nearly laugh at how dumb he looks.

Instead, I explain as briefly as possible. "She told me she lives lakefront on Rubicon Bay. I jokingly asked who she had to divorce to afford it."

"Wow," Paula says.

"Are you a fucking idiot?" Julie asks. "Do you not know who she is?"

"She's Scarlet."

"Who she is *since* high school, you jackass."

"Huh?"

"She's a fucking billionaire, Griffin. Not because she married a rich man, but because she's brilliant. She's like *the* queen of space robotics."

"What?"

"The company she founded three years ago, at the age of twenty-fucking-five, went public last winter with a ninety-billion-dollar valuation. She's been on every thirty-before-thirty list written in the last five years. She was in *Fortune* magazine's "10 Women to Watch" feature. She gave a goddamn *TED Talk*."

"Shit."

"Yeah, buddy, you stuck your foot so far down your throat you'll be shitting it out," Rob adds.

"Thanks." I grumble at him. To Julie I ask, "What's her number? I need to apologize."

"Oh no. If you want to apologize to Scarlet, you'll have to find her yourself. Have your people call her people, or whatever you richies do these days."

I roll my eyes and appeal to Rob and Paula next. But it's clear they're with Julie on this. I've screwed up massively, and I have to make it right on my own.

Huffy and pissed, I stomp outside like a spoiled child and slam myself into my Audi, where I catch my breath as I do exactly as Julie suggested: I reach out to my people. Within five minutes, Tina, my assistant, has not only obtained Scarlet's private number, but she's also found her home address. I consider calling, but if Scarlet is anything like me, she screens calls from unknown numbers. If I want to talk to her, I need to go to her.

I rev my engine and head west, on a mission to make things right. Because, well, she called me her childhood crush. If there is any truth to that, then Scarlet and I need to talk.

## CHAPTER 5
*Scarlet*

I can't believe I let that slip. *Christ*! He's probably laughing at me with his friends, and with my friends, with all the friends. *Poor Scabby Scar* and her pathetic crush on the hottest boy in school. Hilarious.

But Paula and Julie wouldn't do that to me. I don't know why I'm letting this mess with my head so much. It's nothing. *Stop fixating. Focus on something else, anything else.*

I slow the boat, gliding across the lake at well under the speed limit, and let the water soothe my raw nerves. The lake is placid tonight. With the full moon reflecting off the smooth surface, as bright as day, it's like skating on ice. I take a deep breath of the crisp, piney air, letting the calm mood wash over me.

When I reach my dock, I steer to the pilings and tie off. The High-Sierras chill of the evening makes the wooden dock almost painfully cold against my bare feet, but it feels amazing after a long day in the heels that dangle from my fingers.

Motion-activated lights illuminate my way toward shore and up the switchback path that leads from the beach to my estate atop the hill. As I reach the lower deck, I speak to the house, instructing it to open all the doors on the east side. The night is too beautiful to not let in the lake breeze.

"Giles, please open the lakefront doors and brew a pot of coffee," I say to the house.

By the time I reach the main floor and follow the rich scent of coffee into the kitchen, Giles has put the lights on low and opened the glass doors that face the lake. I dump my shoes on the floor and sift through the mail on the kitchen counter as I sip fresh coffee from my steaming "Kiss the Librarian" mug. The mail I get at this address mostly consists of political and philanthropic requests for donation. I set it all aside as I take my coffee to the office on the second floor.

I hardly have time to browse my email inbox before Giles announces, "There's a visitor at the front gate." The screen over the fireplace flickers on to show a scene from *White Knightshade*. Except it's not the show; it's the feed of my front gate camera featuring the show's star standing at the end of my driveway, a silver Audi behind him, peering up into the lens of my security camera.

"Giles, enable audio."

"Audio enabled."

"—and I wouldn't blame you if you never wanted to speak to me again, but I want to say I'm sorry for—" Griffin is mid-sentence as the sound comes through.

"Did you drive here?" I interrupt. "Drunk?"

He pauses for a moment, seeming surprised by my non sequitur question, then he answers, "I've only had one beer tonight."

"How did you find my home?"

"My assistant found your information."

"I'm unlisted."

"I'm sure you are, but it's not hard to find the address for the richest resident on Rubicon Bay."

*Fuck.* "What do you want?"

"I don't expect you to let me in or anything. But I owe you a huge apology."

I don't respond, just watch him shuffle from foot to foot, looking uncharacteristically awkward. It's kind of fun to see Mr. Perfect with his feathers ruffled.

He must realize that my silence is his opportunity to apologize, so he dives in. "First of all, I'm truly sorry for always calling you Scar. I thought it was badass, like you, but I knew you didn't like it and I kept using it anyway, which was shitty. I'm sorry."

*He thought I was badass?* My cheeks heat as my lips tug into a grin.

"And the divorce joke tonight was sexist, lazy, beyond stupid, and not even remotely funny."

Griffin is pretty good at apologizing.

"After you left, your friends schooled me on what you've done since high school; I am incredibly impressed. I'd love to hear all about your work, and I'd like to be friends again, Scarlet. I realize I got things off to a spectacularly bad start, and I won't blame you if you tell me to vacate the premises. But I hope you'll find it in your heart to forgive me and let me buy you dinner. Or, hell, you can buy me dinner. You can afford it."

I cover my mouth to hide my laughter. I can't help it. He's funny, and he's always managed to make me laugh, even when it was at my own expense.

I consider for a long while, letting him wiggle and wait. I look down at the cup of coffee cooling on my desk and feel the pull I always felt when it came to Griffin; a desperate need to be near him.

Work can wait until morning. I grab my phone and press the entrance button. On Griffin's end, there's a soft buzz and click before the driveway gate slowly swings open. He smiles for the camera, then hops into his Audi.

I close the gate behind him and watch on the cameras as

he winds his way up the long driveway to the portico. Every inch of this place is monitored. All it would take is an utterance of my safe words, and Giles would have security responding within twenty seconds.

Not that I'm worried. Griffin was a lot of things in high school, but a creep was never one of them. And that's the sort of thing that doesn't change about a person.

Some things never change, no matter how much a person's life alters. Take my crush on the tall, dark, and handsome man stepping out of his car and approaching my door. That hasn't changed one iota, and probably never will.

I take a fortifying breath and exit my office to greet him.

## CHAPTER 6
*Griffin*

Scarlet's house is spectacular, which is saying something coming from a guy with a mansion in the Hollywood Hills. It's not much bigger than mine, but every detail is perfect. The grounds are dotted with large boulders that form privacy screens to hide the house from the street, and interspersed with the pines are rare towering Sequoia trees, their roots protected from development in this landscape.

The house blends well with its surroundings. Large timber beams form a tall portico over the entrance, but otherwise, the front of the house seems as cozy as a log cabin. When I step up to the glass front door, I catch a glimpse of the mansion's true splendor—the view. The entire back of the house is made of glass. Standing here, I can see all the way to the moonlit lake and the eastern peaks of the Lake Tahoe Basin. But none of that—not the majesty of this mansion nor the breathtaking landscape—can top Scarlet's beauty when she opens the door.

"Hi," she says, her voice sweet and smooth like warm honey.

"Hello," I say back, my voice thick with nervous anticipation.

"Come in." She steps aside.

I enter the lap of luxury. Every detail, from the gleaming marble floors to the dramatic wooden peaks of the ceilings, is so well appointed it looks accidental. It looks like old money; the sort of wealth that comes from a comfort with the lifestyle. But I know Scarlet, and she didn't come from money. Yet here she is, effortlessly stepping into this new world. It is unbelievably interesting to me.

To counter the chill of the back wall of windows standing open to the crisp evening breeze, a fire blazes in the hearth on one wall of the vast room. A gourmet kitchen occupies the opposite wall. And in between, comfortable-looking sofas stretch across the expanse.

"Your home is exceptionally beautiful, Scarlet."

She smiles, and, like her wealth, it looks natural. It's always been like that with her—happiness was so easy. I've worked my whole life to appear happy—I was acting long before I sought to make it my career—so Scarlet's smile always fascinated me. Everything about Scarlet fascinated me, and still does.

Even the mood of her house is effortless. There's a warmth here that my house simply can't achieve, no matter how many designers I hire to transform the space, no matter how many plants my housekeeper adds to the corners.

"Thank you." She shuts the door and walks to the kitchen, her bare feet with red-tipped toes slapping softly against the marble floors. I want to take off my shoes and socks, too, but that would be rude. I have more groveling to do before I can strip off any clothing.

"Would you like some wine?" she asks.

"Sure, but not much. I'm driving, remember?" I follow her to the kitchen and slide onto one of the plush leather stools set at the counter, watching her uncork and pour a bottle of Masseto Merlot. Damn, she's matured into a woman of expensive tastes.

She hands me one of the glasses and leads the way to a

pair of chaise lounge chairs perched on the cliff-side deck. The lights of the hotel casinos on the Nevada side of the lake reflect and shimmer on the surface of the water, but my attention is drawn to the stars overhead.

Like she's thinking the same thing, she says, "Giles, lower the lights," and the house dims behind us so we can see more of the celestial skies.

I jump and nearly spill my wine when a disembodied male voice asks, "Is this satisfactory?"

"Yes, Giles, thank you," Scarlet responds.

I marvel for a moment at the wonder that is Scarlet and her talking house before I realize I recognize the voice.

"Isn't that the guy from *Buffy*?"

She nods at me over the top of her wineglass. "Anthony Stewart Head, yes."

"Holy shit, how did you get him to voice your smart home?"

"He's the voice in my car and office, too, and I...well, I'm not entirely sure what I did was legal, so don't tell anyone."

"What?" I laugh at the thought of Scarlet ever breaking a law.

She cringes. "I didn't actually pay the actor to provide his voice."

"Oh."

"But, I mean, I could. I should. I will. But first I wanted to find out if I could even do it. Giles—"

"Yes, Scarlet?" The house—in the voice of Rupert Giles, the character from *Buffy the Vampire Slayer*, played by the award-winning actor Anthony Stewart Head—asks her.

"Please put on some music, sound level low, and then you may go off-line until I say 'Glorificus.'"

"System off-line," Giles says as the soft sounds of an 80s new-wave song float in the air around us.

"Okay, sorry. I have to put him off-line, or he responds every time I say the word 'Giles.' I send him off-line when I watch *Buffy* re-runs too, because he responds to Willow's voice from the television."

I laugh.

"Anyway, I programmed an AI to record every instance of Giles speaking in each episode of *Buffy*. I isolated his track to eliminate music and background noise, then synthesized and equalized the words, syllables, and tones, and mapped them to a glossary to use for the audio track on my security and lifestyle systems."

"Wow."

"Once a dork, always a dork, right?"

I blink at her. "You were never a dork, Scarlet." She was beautiful and brilliant, with her easy smile and bright green eyes that only hinted at the depth of her intelligence.

She hides her expression behind the rim of her wineglass, but I see the dimple pop in her cheek.

"I'm impressed. Giles Bot is the coolest shit I've heard in a while."

"Thanks. I can do you, too, if you want. If you have a voice-activated AI gadget, I can overwrite the default audio with your voice from episodes of *White Knightshade*."

"Please don't." I laugh so hard I send some woodland creatures skittering through the trees to our left.

Scarlet raises a brow at my appalled response.

"I don't think it's a good idea for me to talk to myself in my house. I do enough of that already."

She stares at me a moment, then changes the subject. "So, big-time Hollywood star, huh? How does it feel?"

I sigh, feeling a weight settle on my shoulders. "Not as great as you might imagine."

"Oh, yeah? Why is that?"

"It's a lot of long hours and too much time spent on the wrong things."

"Like what?"

"Youth and beauty. I've been playing a vampire for seven

years. Despite my best efforts, I don't look like the same vampire who started the detective agency at the beginning of the show."

"I can only imagine how hard it would be to play an immortal character for so many years."

I nod. "The obsession with perpetual youth isn't just a vampire thing. Hollywood is an entire town full of vampires. This season, they've started smoothing out my crow's feet with CGI in post-production."

"Jesus!" She looks upset on my behalf, which feels nice. Then she leans forward, squinting at me. "I don't even see crow's feet."

"On a seventy-inch, high-definition television, you can't miss them." I sound like I'm whining; I need to stop with the negativity. But there is something so genuine in Scarlet's eyes, always has been, and I don't like to act in front of her. The truth is that all I have in me right now is negativity. Before I can stop myself, I blurt out my big secret. "Apparently, the crow's feet were the last straw with the producers. They killed off my character this season."

"What?" She scares off the rest of the woodland creatures with her shriek of surprise.

*Shit.* "That is highly confidential information. I violated my nondisclosure agreement by telling you. I could lose millions of dollars. I'm sure that's chump change to you, but it's a lot of money to me. Please don't share any of this."

"I promise." She zips and locks her lips, then tosses the imaginary key over the deck railing. "But you have to tell me *everything*. Right. Now."

"Do you watch the show?"

"Of course I watch the show, Griff."

*Griff.* As much as Scarlet always hated when I called her Scar, I always loved when she called me Griff. I can't help the dumb smile that slides across my lips at hearing it again. Plus, *she watches my show.*

Leaning in a little closer, I tell her everything. "It's in the season finale, on a full moon like tonight. Belladonna has gone missing, and Darius Nightshade follows a tip that she's in an abandoned warehouse known for werewolf activity on Chicago's south side, but it's a trap. Darius was lured there by Lucian, who is the father of Belladonna's baby—"

"Oh my God!"

"Darius walks into a den of werewolves during a full-moon orgy and gets, well, eaten."

"Oh my God!" She covers her mouth as she giggles. "Oh, Griff, Why am I laughing? I'm so sorry for your loss, but also, it's so absurd."

She's right; it is absurd. I laugh, too, and it feels good. "At least it's a spectacular death."

Her expression sinks and she sighs. "What am I going to watch now? I mean, come on. *White Knightshade* without Darius Nightshade? It sounds like they jumped the shark."

"You really watch the show?"

"I'm a devoted fan." She quickly adds, "I love teenage paranormal drama; you know this."

I nod.

"And I like to see you."

My ego inflates like a goddamn hot-air balloon, but I try not to let it show.

Scarlet drinks a big sip of wine before asking, "So, what's next for you?"

"Good question. That's kind of why I'm here. Trying to discover what I want to do with the rest of my life."

"You don't want to act anymore?"

I shrug. I've been doing a lot of that lately, shrugging. "After high school, I went straight to Hollywood. I didn't necessarily want to *act*. I just wanted to be a star."

"Well, you checked that box."

"Yeah, I guess so. I never loved the work, though. I don't ache to perform some new role."

"What do you ache for?" she asks.

*At the moment, Scarlet, I ache for you.* I clear my throat and take a sip of wine. "I don't know, something creative, maybe writing. In the meantime, I'm having fun hanging out with my nephews. My sister has three boys, and their dad is in China for a trade show, so I'm helping her keep the rascals busy."

"Is that what you want? A family?"

I've been giving that a lot of thought lately. "Yeah, I do."

"Leaving the Hollywood vampires behind to be a dad. That sounds like a good life choice."

"Well, first I have to fall in love. Can't have a family without love." *This conversation is getting weird.* I change the subject, sort of... "Tell me more about you. Do you love what you're doing?"

## CHAPTER 7
*Scarlet*

It doesn't escape my notice that he's said the word "love" three times in the last three seconds, and it doesn't take a genius to spot his rapid subject change.

"Yes, I love what I do."

"Tell me about it," he beckons. "And again, I'm sorry I didn't keep up with you as well as you've kept up with me."

"Well, I wasn't on a hit television series you could tune into every week."

"Still. You were on the cover of *Fortune* magazine."

"Twice." I hold up two fingers and realize how egotistical and drunk that makes me look, so I lower my hand and shrug. "But I don't expect you read *Fortune* magazine."

"Alas, I do not," he winks, and my heart does a little hiccup in my chest, "but my car read the article to me on the drive over. Sounds like you hit the big time."

"If you can call robotics technology and quantum physics the big time, then sure."

He gestures at my house and the view, my little piece of prime-real-estate paradise. Okay, he has a point. I can pretend to be modest, but it's a hard sell in this place.

"Okay. Yes. I hit the big time. I created a company developing an AI system that can independently pilot rover missions to the edges of our solar system and possibly, hopefully, beyond."

"Like the Mars rover?"

"Similar. It will be a self-learning, self-driving unit, but it will be more maneuverable and capable of going much farther than Mars. NASA has contracted us to develop an improved machine learning system that will substantially expand its capabilities. Another team is working on rapid transmission of communication back to Earth, and others are working on propulsion and durable robotics construction for withstanding the extremes of deep space." I take a breath and leave it at that. I always feel like I'm talking too much when I go on about work, having to repeatedly remind myself that my passions bore other people.

Griffin stares intently, the moon hanging low in his iceberg eyes. He's so beautiful. Hollywood is full of idiots if they consider him less captivating at this age. If anything, he's more gorgeous than when the series began. Gone is any semblance of the boy he used to be; Griffin Stone has grown into one hell of a man.

"I'm impressed, but I'm not surprised," he says, and my heart does weird girly gymnastics in my chest. "You've always been amazing. I remember when your dad got you that big telescope. You were always staring at the stars. You'd get all wide-eyed with excitement when you'd talk about it. I've never seen anyone as excited about anything as you were about space."

"Really?"

He nods. "I'd ask you questions about it, and you'd answer in these carefully packaged ways, like you wanted to get me excited about it, too. Like you didn't want to bore me."

"Well, yeah, I frequently bore people when I talk about space and robotics."

"You never bored me. I could listen to you talk for hours."

*What a thing to say.* How do I respond to that? Of course, my brain thinks of the worst thing to say. "Stop. I was a complete dork. You don't have to pretend. I know I was a joke."

"A joke?"

"You and your friends were always making fun of me. *Poor little Scabby Scar, always wishing upon a star.*" I repeat the taunt some of the cheerleaders invented to torment me in the hall outside the science lab.

"Jesus." He shakes his head. "I can't speak for my friends. Some of them were assholes, and I should have done more to stop their bullying. But you were never a joke to me."

"You were always kidding around, too. You'd ask me out, and then you'd laugh about it."

"No." He points at me, accusing. "You'd laugh about it. If I laughed, it was defensive, to save my ego in the face of rejection."

"Rejection?" I guffaw. I don't know why I do it. Maybe it's like he said, a defensive maneuver. "Like that time you asked me to prom, it was—"

"You thought I was joking?"

I blink, a little stunned by the harsh tone of his voice and the confusing nature of his words. "Of course."

"Why would I joke about that?"

I sit up on my chaise and set my feet on the ground in a defensive posture. The wine loosens my tongue, and I say too much, giving a voice to the insecurities I've silently harbored for years. "I don't know, maybe to lure me under a bucket of pig's blood."

"Are you talking about *Carrie*?"

"Yes. It's extreme, I know. Still, I figured you'd lost a bet."

"Jesus. Is that what you thought of me?"

"Kind of…"

"No wonder you treated me like dog shit."

*What?* "I never treated you like dog shit."

"You were literally the only girl in school I wanted to be with, and you laughed at me every time I asked you out. I figured you saw me as a dumb jock, not good enough for you."

Jesus, what alternate universe is this? Despite my red hair, I am not Molly Ringwald. And Griffin is not Jake fucking Ryan. Though, now that I think about it, he kind of looks like Jake Ryan. How is it he's cast our adolescences as the unlikely love story in *Sixteen Candles* while I always imagined the horror fest *Carrie*? "You're kidding, right?"

"No, Scarlet, I'm not kidding. I was never kidding."

Griffin sets his wine aside and stands. He walks to the railing and looks out at the placid lake. His back is to me, but I see how tightly he squeezes the railing, the stiff set of his posture, and how exquisite his ass looks in those jeans.

After a deep breath, he says, "So we're clear: I was desperately in love with you, Scarlet. Every time I asked you out, I was serious. And every time you laughed at me, you broke my heart."

*What?* I shift to my feet, ready to go to him, talk, listen, try to understand how I could have had it so wrong. But when Griffin turns around, he's unrecognizable. This isn't the man I was just talking to. This is the Hollywood version of Griffin, with a fake smile plastered over his handsome features. He claps his hands, an actor starting a scene, and in a tone devoid of emotion, says, "Thank you for the wine. I'm glad we could catch up, Scarlet, but I should go."

And with that, he gives me a stiff bow, then walks through my living room and out of my life. I stand there gaping like a fish. Speechless. Stunned.

*What just happened?*

## CHAPTER 8

*Griffin*

"Catch me!" That's the only warning I get before Lee—the youngest of my three nephews—pounces from the arm of the couch. He lands mostly on my stomach, but one of his knees nails me squarely in the nuts.

"Oh...kay!" I narrowly avoid yelling "shit" at the top of my lungs as pain radiates up my spine. I hug my arms around him while I try to recover and he tries to wiggle free.

It's too early for him to have this much energy, especially considering he's home from school today because he convinced my sister he's sick. Now I'm babysitting the toddler tornado, and I might not survive.

"Sick little boys don't fly like Superman; they mope in a cave like Batman."

"I'm not sick," Lee shouts from the cage of my arms.

I gasp like I'm shocked. "Umm... Did you tell your mom a fib?"

Lee freezes, like he's realized his mistake, then giggles when I tickle him. He knows he can trust me not to tattle on him. It's part of the Uncle Code of Conduct, and I'm a devoted adherent to the Uncle Code.

I let him worm his way free of my arms and vacate his

couch-flight landing site, then amble to the kitchen, desperate for more coffee.

This morning is rough, but last night with Scarlet was rougher. I'd insulted her, but the groveling had been fun. She was finally starting to forgive me, I think, when her insult landed. It still hurts to learn she thought my feelings were a trick, a cruel joke.

*"I was desperately in love with you, Scarlet."* Talk about a knee to the nuts. I feel exposed, vulnerable in ways I haven't known before. I'd sooner agree to strip naked on camera than open myself up like that again.

But Scarlet needs to know the truth. Even if all it does is convince her one less person was mocking her in high school, it feels important to have said it. And, hell, maybe it was an important admission for me, too. Now I can move on. The "one that got away" was never actually on my hook; she wasn't even in the same lake.

The doorbell rings, and Lee darts toward the door like he's going to answer it. I catch him around the waist and carry him with me to the front entry, him wiggling the whole way. With my coffee in one hand and my nephew in the other, I instruct Lee to turn the knob for me. He gets a kick out of that, still giggling like mad when the door swings open to Scarlet standing on my sister's doorstep.

"Uh..." I stand there like an idiot, staring at her as Lee dangles at my side. I sound like an idiot, too, when I wonder aloud, "How did you find—?"

"You're not the only one with staff who know how to locate people." Scarlet shoots me the same mischievous smile she used to wear when she broke some small rule—she never broke any of the big rules. Her gaze bounces between Lee and me. "Is this a bad time?"

*A bad time for what? Why is she here?* My brain is still short circuiting. The sight of her always did this to me. It's weird to feel dumbstruck like this again, after all these years. I finally answer her question without answering it at all. "I'm on sick nephew duty. Isn't that right, Lee? You're *sick*."

The kid has no poker face. He giggles manically, and I set him back on his feet so he can run down the hall toward his bedroom.

"I'm sorry, I shouldn't have turned up like this. I should go—"

"I'm pretty sure Lee is faking," I say. Scarlet furrows her brow. And rightly so, that statement makes no sense without context, so I add, "What I mean is this isn't a plague house or anything. You're welcome to come in…if you like."

She gingerly steps inside, looking at the family photos that line the wall of Tricia and Tao's entry hall.

"Want anything to drink?" I ask, trying to bring my hosting skills back online.

"It's a bit early for me." She frowns.

"I meant coffee or water…"

"Oh." She blushes an adorable shade of pink, like her cheeks are trying to match her hair. "Coffee would be great."

I lead her to the kitchen, and Scarlet takes a seat at the island bar, watching me as I work at the coffee maker. When it's ready, I join her, eager to understand why she's here.

After taking a long, thoughtful sip of her drink, Scarlet finally speaks. "I'm sorry to show up on your doorstep first thing in the morning."

"It's fair, considering where I turned up last night."

She smiles and takes another sip.

"I wanted to—"

"About what I—"

We both pause until I gesture for her to go first.

She sets her mug aside and twists her fingers together, considering, then finally looks me in the eye when she says, "I didn't know you felt that way about me. I mean, you were *the* Griffin Stone, and I was just Scabby Scar."

I grimace, starting to hate that nickname, too.

She adds, "Honestly, I never thought I was better than you. I thought I wasn't good enough."

Nonsense. "Scarlet, you're amazing; you always were."

"Well, I know that...now. But back then, I was an insecure little girl."

Her confidence is so goddamn sexy. "And I was an idiot boy who should have told his friends to shut up." I open my mouth to say more, but Lee comes zooming through the room in his Batman cape. He circles us at the kitchen island over and over, clearly delighted when Scarlet watches him.

*I know the feeling, buddy.* Having Scarlet's attention feels good. It always did. Her easy smile breathes life into me. Like a hibernating bear waking after a long winter, my feelings for her yawn and stretch and fill me up.

On Lee's third trip around the island, I capture him with one arm and hold him above the floor. He weighs a lot less than I bench press, so it's minimal effort for maximum reward when Scarlet laughs at us both, me pestering and tickling my nephew while he tries to run away in midair.

"Will you have dinner with me tonight?" I ask her over Lee's head.

"Uh..." Scarlet blinks once, twice, considering, then answers, "Yes."

I smile wide, and so does she.

## CHAPTER 9
*Scarlet*

We're at the nicest restaurant in town. The one attached to the golf course right on the lake. The one with legendary views of the sunset. One of the many restaurants my family couldn't afford when I was a kid.

For the most part, the novelty of my wealth has worn off. But during the first year after my company's IPO, I'd wanted to do everything I'd been denied before. Having the jet, the boat, the three houses, and money to blow on anything my heart desired meant something to me.

I'd come to this restaurant then, reserving the entire place for an evening. I ate alone while the sun set over the town where I grew up. It was obnoxious, and looking back, I'm embarrassed I did it, but at the time, it felt important. It felt like I'd arrived at the boys' club. Me, a lower-class STEM girl, who hadn't been invited through the front door, busted through the wall like the Kool-Aid Man.

Now, I'm back, and I'm not alone. The entire restaurant watches Griffin and me cross to our table; the same table I'd chosen for myself that night, the best table in the house.

Fancy restaurants and rich men don't impress me anymore. But something about this night at this restaurant with this man has me feeling giddy. My gaze bounces between where the sun's golden rays kiss the top of the mountains across the lake and the timber beams that soar overhead. I'm fascinated by how the ceiling's undulating design mimics the peaks and valleys of the surrounding landscape.

Griffin helps me with my chair before settling into his, and when he does, I focus entirely on him. He looks devastatingly handsome, every inch the Hollywood heartthrob in a tailored black suit with a crisp white shirt beneath. But when he grins at me, I see the boy I remember. I bite my lip to keep from giggling like the girl I used to be.

"You look surprisingly impressed," Griffin says.

"I guess I am. Growing up in this town without money had a lasting impact."

"And now you could buy this place without blinking an eye."

I hate talking about money.

Griffin must sense that. He changes the subject. "How are your parents doing? Mitch and Stefanie, right?"

I didn't know he knew my parents' names, let alone remembered them. "They're good. They're outside Phoenix now, enjoying desert life. How about your family?"

He grins, but it doesn't reach his eyes. "Well, you met Lee. He's one of three boys, so Tricia has her hands full. But she and Tao have a good thing going. Mom is doing well. She downsized to a retiree condo in Incline Village and loves it there. Dad died."

"Oh. I'm sorry."

Griffin opens his mouth and closes it, then simply says, "Mom's happier now."

What a sentence. He's packed so much into those three words. Before I can dissect the myriad of meaning, the server brings our wine and takes our order.

When he's gone, Griffin's demeanor is entirely changed;

he's the actor acting. He smiles so beautifully, and the waning light of the day highlights the strong lines of his face. "Tell me about you, Scarlet. I want to know everything."

It's clear the last subject is closed. So I do. I go into detail about how StarReach was born and the day we successfully tested our first prototype, share amusing stories of venture capital fundraising, and conclude with the IPO last year.

I take my time, leaving ample opportunity for him to interrupt and talk about himself. He never does. After working with boardroom alphas for years, it's discombobulating to speak to a man who isn't desperate to flex his intellect in front of me.

But then I remember what he said last night. "*I figured you saw me as a dumb jock, not good enough for you.*" Maybe he thinks he doesn't have an intellect to flex. That makes me sad. Griffin isn't dumb. He never was. Tutoring him had been easy because he understood all the concepts. He just had a hard time focusing.

But now, he focuses...on me. Now I'm the one feeling those old insecurities. I sound like a braggart, going on and on about myself. Why doesn't he interrupt me? My food is getting cold. I'm ready to eat and listen for a while. My confidence wavering, I pause to take a long sip of wine.

Finally, he speaks. "I'm impressed, Scarlet. You've always known what you wanted, and you reached out and grabbed it. And now you're a billionaire. I can't even wrap my head around how much money that is."

"Well, to be fair, that's my net worth. It's not like I have a billion dollars in my bank account. Not that my bank account is anything to scoff at, but the bulk of my wealth comes from my shares of StarReach."

"Star..." He muses, looking so intently into my eyes I can't bear to blink or look away. "That should have been your nickname all those years ago. Scarlet the Starlet."

I grimace.

"Okay, not Starlet, just Star."

"Like in *The Lost Boys*?"

He laughs. "I'm no good at this, am I?"

"At what?"

"Flirting."

"Is that what you're doing?"

He holds his hand to his chest like I've wounded him. "Yeah, it's been years since I had to try." He pauses to consider. "In fact, I think the last time I had to try was with you. And I failed miserably."

I try not to laugh, fail. Still, I'm not loving this image of myself. "You make me sound like hard work, like I'm a job."

"You are." He smirks. "But any job worth doing is worth doing right."

*Oh. Kay.* My mind, or rather my body, fixates on the way Griffin says, "worth doing right." A tingle travels down my spine to settle between my legs, warm and needy.

I clear my throat awkwardly and return my attention to my food, eating with determined focus. I glance over at Griffin, who's grinning at me like he knows exactly where my head's at, but he says nothing.

When we finish the meal, we savor coffee for dessert. We're lingering, neither of us wanting this night to end, but the sun has set, and the restaurant needs to turn over the table. So when he suggests, "How about a walk along the water?"

I'm quick to agree, "I'd love that."

# CHAPTER 10
*Griffin*

Scarlet leans on my shoulder to step out of her heels, and the breeze blows a few tendrils of her strawberry-scented hair against my cheek.

I take a deep breath. God, I didn't know how much I'd missed her. For a year of my life, she was a constant presence. I'd see her in class, and then she'd visit my house a couple times a week. I hadn't realized until now, but those moments were the highlight of my senior year.

Now, talking to her again, staring at her unabashedly, laughing with her, making her blush, it's a gift. Every minute I spend with her makes me want a thousand minutes more.

I want to wrap my arms around her and press my lips to hers, to know her taste and the sounds of her gasps and sighs and screams. I want it all. But this is a first date, and I need to slow my roll. I royally screwed up my first shot with her; I will not screw this one up, too.

So I let her balance on me as she steps out of her shoes and flexes her toes in the cool sand. She shivers, and I use it as an excuse to slip my jacket off and drape it over her shoulders. She tries to hide it, but I notice when she breathes in my scent from the lapel.

We make our way across the soft sand of the beach. Overhead, the moon hangs heavy in the sky, and a breeze whispers through the needles of the pines, creating a hush I've missed since moving to LA.

It is a perfect night. The sunset, the warmth of spring, the wine coursing through my veins to relax me, and Scarlet's company: it's all so...perfect.

I'm surprised by how comfortable I feel right now. In high school, I was always on edge around her. But I was on edge in general back then. For years, I've been keyed up like a runner ready to race, always chasing something. Whether I was seeking an escape from my father, fame and fortune on the silver screen, or the latest and greatest accolades. But right here, right now, I feel like I've found what I've been searching for. I can finally stop running.

Scarlet comes to a stop and turns her head up to the sky, watching as the first stars prick through the dusky veil, and I stop to watch her. She is stunning, truly extraordinary, and she's the only person who's ever managed to capture my attention so completely.

"Starlet," I whisper.

Scarlet pulls her gaze from the heavens to look at me. Her smile fades when we lock eyes; it's replaced by a curious expression, and her eyes burn with a heat I haven't seen before. We freeze, waiting, like we're on the verge of something.

The breeze ruffles her hair and sends a strand fluttering across her cheek, tangling in the sooty arch of her eyelashes. I delicately stroke those wayward strands behind her ear, then keep my hand there.

With my palm cupping the side of her face, my thumb stroking her cheek, and my pinky resting against her pulse point, I feel the flutter of her heart racing and the jagged shudder of her breath when I touch her.

Scarlet leans into me a little. I lean into her a lot. I long for the press of her lips against mine. It's what I've ached for since we were sixteen and sitting inches apart in English class. Back then, she was always out of my reach. Now, I have her in my grasp.

"I want to kiss you." My voice is quiet enough for the wind to blow my words away, but loud enough I know she heard me.

Scarlet's lashes flutter, and she wets her lips with the tip of her tongue. I wrap my fingers around the back of her neck, pulling her closer. I'm desperate now, but still, I wait. If we're going to start something, I need it to be Scarlet who leads the way.

Like she can read my mind, she shifts onto the toes of her bare feet and kisses me. My breath stalls in my lungs; my heart stops in my chest: I die a little death. And then, just as suddenly, I come alive, reborn. Heat races through my veins, my heart pounds like it's fighting to escape my chest, and my lungs drag in her scent, nourishing every cell in my body with her essence.

God, the softness of her, the sweetness. I need so much more than a taste. With a deep moan, I angle my mouth over hers and consume her with my kiss, devouring her rich merlot flavor. She moans, too, and the sound feeds my hunger.

Lately, I've wondered what I should do with my life, and now I have my answer. I want to kiss Scarlet for the rest of my days.

I wrap my arms around her and lift her off her feet, holding her tight. She loops her arms around my neck and laces her fingers in my hair. Gasping for air, we eventually come apart to catch our breath.

"I've wanted to do that for as long as I can remember," I admit.

"Me, too." Scarlet presses her forehead against mine. "I'm sorry I hurt you, Griffin. I didn't know."

"I know. I'm sorry, too."

"I let my insecurity blind me—"

"Shh—" I kiss the tip of her nose. "Let's let it go. This thing between us isn't about the past anymore, is it?"

She shakes her head.

"Thank God." I kiss her again, this time a little slower, sweeter. I kiss her like we have all the time in the world, and this is how we've chosen to spend it. And, if I have any say in the matter, we will.

## CHAPTER 11
*Scarlet*

I slept late for probably the first time in eight years, and it was glorious. Everything is glorious today. Last night, Griffin kissed me. Though to call what we shared last night a kiss is a gross understatement.

From the beach, we walked to the pier and onto my boat, where we sat on the deck for hours, lulled by the gentle sway of the water, staring up at the stars, talking a little, and kissing a lot. It was my teen dream come true.

And, despite Griffin's assertion that we're letting the past go and starting over, the more time I spend with him, the more memories from our past surface. Kindnesses that, at the time, I explained away. Now I can see them for what they are: Griffin's sweetness. Like the time he bought me a cupcake and put a candle in it on my birthday. Jesus, talk about a *Sixteen Candles* moment. But I was so wrapped up in my head, so tangled and twisted in my insecurities, I missed it. I missed so much. But no more.

Griffin is right. The past is then and this is now. We're not the same people we were; we can communicate now, connect now. We can have lots and lots of sex now. That's all I've been able to think about since Griffin stepped off my boat last night with one lingering kiss goodnight.

I know I'm not alone in my wicked thoughts. I saw the hungry look in his eyes each time he kissed me. But, unlike the men I've been with—always reaching, grabbing, groping for more—Griffin never pushed. I've never wanted a man's hands on me more, and the promise of that is making me giddy today. It's like I've reverted to my teenage self, a bubbly little girl all hopped up on romance and naive optimism. It's a bit embarrassing, but it's fun to be boy crazy again.

I sip my coffee on the deck and watch the lake reflect the late morning light, shimmering like silver sequins. The sight is enrapturing, too beautiful to fully comprehend. Setting my steaming mug on the railing, I stretch my arms over my head. My body feels good this morning, lighter and freer than it has in years. But that's how I feel about everything this morning. My sheets were so soft I kept scissoring my legs to feel the silkiness caress my skin. My coffee is so rich I savor it with a moan.

Off to my left, I hear a sound that reminds me of Griffin, like the growl he makes right before he takes my mouth with a hot, wet kiss. It's a hungry, grumbly noise that sends a shiver of excitement through me. Except...Griffin isn't here, so who—or what—is making the noise?

I glance to the end of the deck, where a cluster of tall pine trees provides privacy from neighbors. And there among the low-slung boughs is a face. No... Wait... This can't be real. There can't be a black bear climbing from one of the trees to the railing of my deck. Right? That's absurd.

The bear watches me as my brain tries to process what I'm seeing. He seems as surprised to find me here as I am to find him in my tree, stepping onto my railing.

I take a step back and the bear moves, too. The copse of trees shakes as he shifts his weight to the deck.

Jesus, he's big. I keep assuming the bear is a male, but I have no idea how to determine its sex. Is that the most important thing to fixate on right now, brain? Considering there is a giant *fucking* bear standing not more than twenty feet away from me?

*What in the hell do I do?*

I have a stratospheric IQ, plus I grew up here, so I'm no stranger to bear safety considerations, but in this moment, I'm struck dumb. My fight-or-flight response is going haywire, because I know I shouldn't run from a bear, but I'm not supposed to fight with it either. There is no reasoning with me right now, and the moment that bear stands to his full height, my blood goes cold, and my feet get fleet.

I run. Turning toward the open-plan living room/kitchen combo, I dart for the hallway to my bedroom on the south side of the house, putting as much distance between me and the bear as I can.

My bare feet smack the marble floors as I sprint. Behind me, the sounds of crashing, shattering, and grunting suggest the bear is in hot pursuit. He's fast, and he quickly closes the distance I try to put between us.

"Giles!" I scream at the house. "Shut all the doors now! This is an emergency."

Giles gets right to work. However, the mechanisms that close the window-walls on the lake side of the house are not programmed for speed in an emergency. They unfold at a maddeningly slow pace, and the bear follows me inside before the walls can close behind me.

Fuck! Now I've trapped myself in the house with a fucking bear. The sound of the lumbering beast follows me up the long hallway, and I catch a glimpse of him reaching my bedroom door as I sprint to the closet, which doubles as a panic room. I slam the closet door shut and press all my weight against it just as he reaches for me. The door trembles and quakes as the bear's claws slash the mahogany.

"Parker Abrams is a poophead!" I shout the absurd *Buffy* reference like a crazy person—please, God, don't let those be my last words.

The safe words do the trick. Within seconds, Giles locks down the panic room, a massive steel door sliding shut to close me in. This room is fireproof and intruder safe, and it seems to be bearproof, too. The big guy grumbles and claws at the door, but he can't get to me and eventually loses interest.

I take a deep breath, trying to still my trembling hands as I order the house to call security.

Momentarily, a voice echoes through the small steel room. I recognize the man's voice, Officer Thomas Dennison, the head of my private security team. "Ms. Branson, what is the nature of your emergency dispatch?"

"There's a bear in the house."

"There's a—"

"Bear in the house. Yes, you heard me correctly," I interrupt, hoping to speed up his thought processing. I've had a few additional seconds to overcome the absurdity of this moment, so I use that extra time to take charge from my bunker. "Notify police and request animal control for extraction. Please instruct them to use non-lethal means if possible." I don't want anyone shooting a bear in my house.

There's another pause, like he's trying to determine what code this emergency warrants in the dispatch system.

"I've made it to safety in the panic room. I am in no immediate danger. I just need them to relocate the bear to his natural habitat."

Finally, Officer Dennison gets with the program and responds. "Of course, Ms. Branson. Right away."

"Also, please inform the landscaping team they will need to remove the cluster of trees closest to the house on the north side. The bear scaled them to gain access to the deck."

"Yes, Ms. Branson, of course."

With the end of our transmission, I settle onto the stool in front of my security monitors and watch from the various cameras throughout the house as the black bear sniffs around the living room, relieves himself on my Calacatta marble floor, and goes to the pantry, shredding the door as he hunts for food.

# CHAPTER 12
*Griffin*

I wake to the chorus of "Lucky Man" by The Verve, the ringtone I assigned to Scarlet's number last night after I snuck into my sister's house. I smile as I answer, but the expression vanishes the moment Scarlet speaks.

"There's a bear in my house."

"What?" I'm up. I'm awake. I leap out of bed, confused and circling, half naked, in the center of my sister's guest room.

"He climbed up a tree and chased me into the house. He's in the kitchen now, eating all my food."

"Where are you?"

"In my panic room."

"Are you safe? Are you unharmed?"

"Yes. I'm okay."

I suck in a breath of relief. "Have you called the police?"

"Yes, they're out in the yard strategizing with animal control about how to get the bear out of my house."

I shove my legs into jeans and my feet into sneakers. I tug on a tee and head for the door, waving at my sister and the kids and explaining an emergency has come up. Outside, I run. I go right past my car, racing toward the marina a few blocks away.

Breathless, I talk to Scarlet, hoping to soothe her nerves as I soothe my own. But I hate this helpless feeling, wanting to be there with her, instead of on the phone listening to the woman I'm coming to believe is the one true love of my life tell me she's trapped in her home with a goddamn bear.

At the marina, I look for the boat rental kiosk, but there's a line of waiting customers. Up a ways, a group of young women is loading a cooler onto a bowrider. I run the length of the dock to them, asking as I approach, "Ladies, may I trouble you for a lift to Rubicon Bay as quickly as possible, please?"

"Ohmygod! Ohmygod! Ohmygod!"

"Aren't you Darius Nightshade?"

"It's Griffin Stone!"

"Ohmygod! Ohmygod! Ohmygod!"

They all talk at once, fangirling incoherently. *This was a bad idea.* I glance around, noticing a man carrying a beer cooler toward an old fishing boat.

"Yes, we can take you across the lake in exchange for a photo," one of the women says when she sees me eyeing other options.

"Deal." I hop on board, and the one in charge instructs her friends to untie us from the dock, then guides the boat away from the marina.

"Scarlet," I say into the phone I've had to my ear the whole time. "I'm on my way. I'll be there in fifteen minutes. Hang tight."

Once we hit the channel, Meghan, the boat's owner, hits the throttle. We bounce over crystal blue waves, and the shore smears past us, but it feels like we're inching through mud.

Eventually, we reach the shore to the west, and I direct Meghan to Scarlet's dock. I'm ready to disembark the moment we reach the jetty, but the women demand their photograph.

I lose precious moments posing for at least a dozen photos before cutting the fan convention short and sprinting up the dock. I zig zag up a winding rocky path to the top of the hill and keep an eye out for bears. When I get to Scarlet's house, I make my way around to the front where cops and wildlife rescue personnel aim tranquilizer guns at me like I'm a momma bear looking for her cub. I hold up my hands and beg them not to shoot.

They lower their weapons, and I take several deep breaths to slow my heart rate as I look around at the scene. Lights flash from every vehicle—it looks like several departments have responded, their cars and trucks clogging her circular drive.

The wooden double doors open like they mark the grand entrance to a ball, and several people in forestry uniforms wheel a cart through with a large black bear passed out on it. The bear is skinny—fresh out of hibernation, but massive. One paw hangs limp off the side of the cart and looks about as big as my head. I imagine the kind of damage that paw could have done to Scarlet, and my knees nearly give out.

That's when I see her. She comes out into the sunlight, flanked by two men in dark suits who must be her private security.

Scarlet looks like a chaotic mess, a precious and perfect chaotic mess. Her hair is a wild nest of red curls around her ghostly white face, and she's in her pajamas with a silver emergency blanket clutched around her shoulders. My weak knees are strong again as I run the rest of the distance between us and wrap her in my arms.

She shivers against me, and I hug her even tighter, cupping my palm to the back of her head and kissing her forehead. Relief, that's what this feeling is. I'm so goddamn relieved to have her in my arms again, alive and whole.

That's when it hits me: she called me. In the midst of a traumatic life experience, Scarlet called me. It's heady to know I'm the person she thought of when she needed someone to come to her, to be with her. I take great comfort in that and tuck my face into the softness of her hair, breathing in the strawberry scent.

Together, we watch the animal control officers wrangle the sleeping bear into a sturdy cage on the back of one of their trucks. This is clearly not their first bear rodeo.

Several police officers jog past us toward the front gate to corral onlookers who have ventured onto Scarlet's property to see what the commotion is about. Among the dog-walking neighbors and the five young women I left behind in the boat are a pair of photographers clicking away.

*Terrific.* "Shit."

"What?" Scarlet stares up at me with red-rimmed eyes.

"Paparazzi."

Scarlet looks toward the growing crowd and groans when a television reporter and cameraman sprint as fast and as far as they can up the driveway before the police officers hold up their arms to stop them. One shouts questions at us as the camera lens captures every moment of our embrace.

"Get them off the property," Scarlet says to one of the men in the dark suits, and he quickly directs several other men in black to assist the police in reminding the trespassers to leave.

Amid the flashing strobes and clicking shutters of cameras, Scarlet takes my hand and leads me inside her home, shutting the door on the world outside.

# CHAPTER 13
*Scarlet*

The house is a disaster. In the kitchen, shards of wood and glass litter the floor. Boxes and bags of food are torn apart, their contents eaten or scattered to the four corners. Claw marks gash the front of my stainless-steel fridge. There's scat and urine on the floor where the bear relieved himself.

But I can't think about any of that; my mind is still choking on the last dregs of panic. Gripping Griffin's hand like a lifeline, I lead him into my bedroom where the deep gashes in my closet door are a morbid reminder of how close those claws came to me. I stare at the destruction, and another hiccup of fear bubbles out of me. I came within inches of evisceration. The panic room saved my life today.

I turn away and bury my face against Griffin's chest, taking a deep breath of his scent. He always smelled so good, nothing fake or perfumed, just soap and his natural aroma. His closeness and warmth comfort me, and I cling to him. Griffin wraps his arms around me, and I melt into him, releasing the heavy weight of my anxiety.

Slowly, he leads me to the bed, and I lie down. He joins me, opening his arms again for me to curl against him. I hadn't realized how tired I was, but as the last of the adrenaline drains out of me, I can hardly keep my eyes open. I don't even have the energy to thank Griffin for coming so quickly before I'm out like a light.

∼

A tickling sensation stirs me from my sleep. I open my eyes to find I'm still clinging to Griffin, my hands clutching fistfuls of his shirt and his breath causing my hair to flutter. Another soft exhale warms the top of my head, and the relaxed rhythm of his breathing tells me he's immersed in a deep sleep.

Okay. So now we've slept together. Not in the figurative sense; in the literal one. And it happened a lot quicker than I anticipated.

But nearly being eaten by a bear can have a dramatic impact on a person's priorities. After the morning I've had, sleeping with Griffin rocketed to the top of my to-do list.

Today, I needed comfort, and Griffin dropped everything to give it to me. But he gave me so much more. When Officer Dennison and his colleagues escorted me out of the house behind the tranqed bear, Griffin ran to me. The worry in his expression had a profound effect on me. In that instant, to that man, I felt precious, loved. Falling into his arms and knowing he would hold me up was a foreign and extraordinary feeling.

I've done a lot in my life, and I've done it all on my own. I had the support of my parents, of course, and a few close friends. But every time I walked into a boardroom or a venture capital pitch meeting, I did it alone. I had to psych myself up or calm my own nerves or remind myself that I'm a badass scientist and businesswoman. The thought of relying on someone else for support feels strange and new…and exciting.

I unclench my fists from Griffin's shirt and grimace at the

wrinkles I've made. As I try to smooth them out, his cool aqua eyes flutter open and he blinks a few times. Maybe, like I did when I first woke, he's piecing together the memories of how he ended up in my bed.

"Feeling better?" he asks as he strokes my back and rests a hand on my cheek.

I nod and shift to get closer to him, sliding higher so I can reach his mouth. When I kiss him, he freezes. But that only lasts an instant before he groans and cinches his arms around me, pulling me tight against him, delivering a toe-curling kiss.

Griffin rolls us until I'm beneath him on the bed, letting me feel the weight and strength of his hard body across mine. I pull at the bottom of his shirt, and he severs the kiss long enough to yank it off over his head.

I revel in the feel of him, tracing my fingers over every inch of hard muscle bearing down on me and those statuesque biceps caging me in. I want more. The beast who attacked me is long forgotten, and all I can think about is this beast above me. Safe now in Griffin's arms, I'm desperate for him.

I yank my shirt over my head, all elbows like a bumbling teenager in the back seat of a car. Griffin's eyes spark with fire as he watches me reveal myself to him, then his mouth comes down on one of my nipples, teasing me with his tongue and teeth, driving me wild.

Wiggling my hips impatiently, I long for more. I want the rest of him. My fingers fumble with the button on his jeans, and when I can't get it open, I pull and tug at the denim like I want to tear them off him.

Griffin lets out a deep, rumbly laugh against my chest, and I feel the vibration everywhere. "Slow down, Scarlet. We have all the time in the world."

No. We don't. Doesn't he know I almost died today? Life and death hurtled at me in the blink of a bear's eye, and I wasn't ready. I have plans and ideas, places to go, things to do. And right now, there is this one thing I *really* want to do. I tangle my fingers tighter in his pants, tugging and yanking at the button and zipper.

"Hey, take a breath." Griffin's voice is too calm, too relaxed.

It makes me crazy. I whimper when he pulls away, and my nipples, wet and straining from his mouth, feel cold and exposed. He captures my hands in his, laces our fingers together, and stretches across the top of me, pinning my hands to the mattress over my head. "You're safe now. You're safe with me."

I struggle like I want to get free, but with his weight on me again, I have the safety and warmth I need. Slowly, I allow myself to let go of some of the tension still coiled tight inside.

"Look at me, Star," *Star*. It sends a shiver through me as he whispers his new name for me and brushes soft kisses over my lips. "I've wanted you for as long as I can remember, and I'm not going to rush this. We're going to take our time together. Okay?"

With that, he presses the hard length of his denim-clad cock against my core, and I moan, my desperation only deepening. But when he kisses my breath away, I give in to whatever long, languorous torture he has planned.

He kisses down my body, his mouth and hands returning to my breasts. He teases gently, sending waves of warm arousal through me. Then he pinches and nibbles, and I writhe like a woman possessed.

Griffin looks up at me through the valley between my breasts, a wicked grin on his face. He's driving me mad and he knows it. I rake my fingernails through his hair, feeling a flush of satisfaction when his eyes roll back in his head. At least I won't be the only one going mad here.

With a wink, Griffin turns his gaze back to my body, shifting lower. He curls his fingers into the waist of my yoga pants and strips me out of them, along with my underwear. He kisses his way down my legs as he goes and kisses a path back up again once he has me naked. I spread my legs when he reaches my thighs, earning a chuckle from him, like he's surprised by my boldness.

The girl he once knew was shy. I'm not her anymore, and it's time for him to catch up. I guess that's what he's doing when he stops to stare at me like I'm a masterpiece in a museum.

Frustrated, I huff and shift my legs as if to close them. He grabs my thighs and holds them open, keeping plenty of room there for his shoulders.

"This is where I've always longed to be."

*What?*

"I've wanted you for so long. There's a part of me that can't believe I'm here with you now, and another part is convinced this is where I've always belonged."

*Is he talking to me or my vagina?* As if to clear up my confusion, he gets up on his hands and knees and crawls over my body to deliver a scorching kiss that has me gasping and angling for more as he kisses back down my body.

Clutching my thighs at his ears, Griffin Stone proceeds to eat my pussy like it's his last meal. The first stroke of his tongue has me arching off the bed. He curls his arms around my thighs to keep me still while he flattens his tongue over my folds again and takes another taste.

"God, Star, you're perfect," he mumbles against me as his tongue darts out to tease my clit. I moan and gasp and wiggle, but he holds me tightly against his face as he presses his tongue inside me, making slow penetrations that only hint at what's to come.

"You're so wet," he says when he replaces his tongue with a finger, reaching deeper, curling inside me. "You're so ready for me, aren't you, baby?"

"Yes, please." I beg and moan and writhe, tangling my fingers in his hair, trying to pull him up to me.

He resists. "Come for me first. Give me what I want, Star, and I'll give you what you need." To emphasize his point, he presses two fingers inside me as he teases with his tongue.

"Oh God!" I say, or maybe I don't. I'm not thinking straight and probably not speaking coherently either.

I am so close, ready to explode at the slightest shift in Griffin's pace or pressure. Like he can sense it, he's holding me here, right on the edge, teasing me with so much pleasure, yet no release.

I'm about to complain when he sucks my clit between his lips and fucks me harder and faster with his fingers. I break apart, screaming and writhing in ecstasy. Giving him exactly what he wants, my cries echo in the rafters above the bed.

When I'm limp and still spasming from the aftershocks, I look down to find Griffin watching me from between my legs, his ice-blue eyes burning with desire. His lips, still wet with my flavor, are curled into a self-satisfied smile.

## CHAPTER 14
*Griffin*

Bringing this woman to orgasm is more gratifying than anything I've ever known. Scarlet practically levitates off the bed while screaming my name, and her nails dig into my scalp as she pulls my hair and scissors her legs around my shoulders.

*Goddamn.*

As she comes down, she lies there, blissful and boneless. But only for a moment before she's moving on me. She sits and pulls her legs under her as she tugs at my shoulders to get me to come up onto my knees, too. When we're both kneeling on the bed, she wraps her arms around my neck and pulls me in for a kiss, not at all bothered that my lips are still coated in her come.

I tangle my fingers in her hair to hold her to me, kissing her like she's the air I breathe and I'll die without her. While I do that, her fingers work their way down my chest to the button and fly of my jeans.

That screaming orgasm must have cleared her head because instead of tugging at the denim like she wants to tear my pants off, Scarlet manages to unbutton my jeans the proper way. Though there is nothing *proper* about the way she reaches inside and grabs my cock.

Her hands are so warm it's like she's burning me with her touch. I hiss with pleasure and grit my teeth to keep from coming early like a hormonal teen. She doesn't make it easy for me when she pulls away from my kiss and angles down to suck my cock deep into her eager mouth.

I gasp. Her hands were warm, but, Christ, I'm going to melt in her mouth. She sucks me all the way to the hilt, then strokes her tongue along the length as she pulls back, letting me go with a juicy pop of her lips.

Scarlet looks up at me from there, teasing me with the tip of her tongue before saying, "I'm glad I didn't give my virginity to you."

*What*? She sucks me deep again, and my brain turns to mush. *What was she saying*?

With another pop, my cock bounces free from her lips, and she adds, "Having other men allows me to better appreciate what you have to offer, Griffin."

Scarlet rubs her cheek against my cock, almost cuddling with it. It's a little freaky, and it turns me on. I tenderly rub her other cheek with my palm, like this is romantic.

She settles back a few inches to stare my cock straight in the eye, and says, "Your penis is beautiful, Griffin. Just like you."

*Uh*. Before I can respond, she sucks me deep, and "oh fuck" is all I can manage to say.

My knees wobble, but she holds me up, pushing my jeans farther down my thighs so she can clutch my ass to steady me. I groan as she pricks her nails into my flesh and swirls her tongue around the head, then deep throats me again.

Jesus Christ, Scarlet is good at this. If she doesn't stop, I'll pop off in her mouth.

As much as it pains me, I pull away and step backward off the end of her bed so I'm out of reach. I hurriedly dig through my pockets as I strip out of the rest of my clothes. I don't have a condom. I left the house in such a hurry, I didn't bring my wallet or keys or a "just in case" prophylactic.

Like she can read my mind, Scarlet crawls to the edge of the bed and pulls a box of condoms out of the nightstand drawer. She tears one off and crawls back over to me. Balancing on her knees, she gently rolls the latex on.

When her work is finished, she keeps one hand wrapped around my cock as she looks up at me. Her cheeks are pink with arousal, her eyes dark with desire where her pupils are blown wide, and her silky red curls are mussed from my groping hands.

God, she's gorgeous, and she's mine. I meant what I said before. This is where I've always belonged. Scarlet and I, we were once star crossed, but the stars have aligned to bring me home to her, and her home to me.

Scarlet pulls me down on top of her on the bed, and I go willingly. Balancing on my elbow to keep from crushing her, I cradle her cheek in my palm as I kiss her, delivering in that kiss every promise I haven't yet made to her, but I will.

She moans into my mouth as I ease inside her. Her core tightens around my length with each inch I press deeper. When I'm fully seated, she winces like I'm too large, so I hold myself completely still and wait for her to make the first move.

Soon, Scarlet starts to shift, pulling her hips back and pushing deeper. And with that, I start my own give and take. She lets out the sexiest moan when I pull out nearly to the tip and push back in a little faster and harder.

This feels too good, too perfect. I shake with anticipation, so close to the edge. I shift up onto my knuckles for better movement and a deeper angle. Scarlet matches me stroke for stroke as I build a steady rhythm between us. With each press of our hips, I accelerate until I'm fucking her with every ounce of energy I have.

Sweat slicks between us. It beads on Scarlet's forehead and dampens the strands of her hair as her body moves with mine in perfect sync. God, this is hot, literally. She's like a live wire, sparking, setting fire to everything she touches. And I'm desperate to burn with her.

Scarlet's moans and gasps grow louder and more desperate with our relentless rhythm. Then she freezes, but I keep fucking her as the ecstasy rolls through her in waves. The orgasm dawns in her eyes before she clamps them shut. It tightens her muscles until she bows up to me, her hard nipples sliding across my slick chest. Her nails dig into my back, and her legs tangle so tightly around my hips it nearly stills me, but not…quite…yet…

*Fuck.* I come, too. Heart pounding so vigorously it feels like it'll hit my ribs, I bellow and gasp for air while I ride out the most intense orgasm of my life. I manage a few more strokes to extend our aftershocks, then collapse.

I'm beyond spent. It's like I've hollowed myself out and given it all to Scarlet. She wraps her arms and legs around me, hugging me so tightly against her it's difficult to catch my breath. Tracing her fingers up and down my spine, she tickles my over-sensitized skin until I'm laughing and spasming all over, and she's giggling like mad.

God, this is good. As much as I don't want to admit it, I'm glad I didn't give her my virginity either. This first experience with Scarlet is exponentially better than my first experience with sex was. I'm glad she was spared that and will only ever know my A-game.

Still, I feel like I've missed out. But where do I even start making up for all the lost time between us? I eye the condom box and vow I will wear the rest of those rubbers before this night is over.

For now, I'm content to lie here with her. I curl onto my side and bring her with me, cradling her in my arm. Scarlet smiles sweetly, pushing some of the sweat-soaked hair off my brow, and I do the same for her.

I want to lay it all out there. She should know I'm in love with her, and I always have been. Even when I went on without her, that feeling never went away. My entire adult life, I think I've been waiting for her to come back to me.

But when I open my mouth to say the words, it seems too soon. So I just kiss her forehead and whisper, "This is heaven. Let's never leave."

"There's bear scat on the floor," Scarlet replies.

I raise a brow at her.

"Eventually it's going to smell up the house. We should clean it up."

"I know a great housekeeping service." I reach for my phone and dial the number of the service my sister uses.

While it rings, Scarlet speaks to the house. "Giles, allow the cleaning service inside the front door when they arrive. Access to the main house only. Password is 'blondie bear' to expire at six p.m. tonight."

"Understood," Giles replies.

I relay the pertinent details to the cleaning service, and when I'm off the phone, I curl back up with Scarlet. "Blondie bear, I know that reference."

"Well, Spike has always been my favorite character on *Buffy*."

"I remember."

She looks at me for a long moment before saying, "You actually paid attention to me, didn't you?"

"Of course I did."

"I didn't see it at the time, but I do now. Remember the time you sang Spike's song from the musical episode to me?"

How could I forget? Does she really remember it though? Does she remember the lyrics to Spike's song, "Let Me Rest in Peace"? It's all about the pain of unrequited love. Scarlet's expression falls as I imagine she's working it out in her head. She strokes my cheek, real regret shining in her eyes.

Not wanting to bring the mood down, I change the subject. "I watched that show because you liked it. But it turned out to be a benefit to my career, too. One of the casting agents for *White Knightshade* was a huge *Buffy* fan and flipped her shit when I did Spike's monologue to Buffy and Angel at the Magic Box. I'm fairly sure it landed me the role."

"Oh, well, now you have to do the monologue for me."

It doesn't take much more than a flutter of her eyelashes to convince me. I spring out of bed, toss the condom in the toilet, and return to pace the room, stark naked, as I run through the lines in my head. When I have it, I huff out a breath, curl my lip to take on Spike's persona, and in the character's cockney accent I launch straight into the scene.

When I finish, Scarlet comes onto her knees, clapping and hooting as she wraps her arms around my neck, dragging me back to bed. "Oh my God, you're an amazing Spike, and I'm extremely turned on right now," she says as she pushes me to my back and climbs on top.

## CHAPTER 15
*Scarlet*

It's early when my phone pings with a text from my assistant, Maria: WHY DIDN'T YOU TELL ME YOU WERE DATING GRIFFIN STONE?!?!

What? I drowsily read the text a couple of times while the three little dots at the bottom of the messaging window blink.

Finally, her follow-up comes through: AND YOU WERE ATTACKED BY A BEAR!?!

I stare at the words, not sure how to reply to either message. Another ping sounds when she pastes the link to a tabloid article in the text.

I gasp at the photo, which pops up at the top of the page. Griffin stirs beside me and laces his arm around my waist, sleepily cuddling closer.

The photo is weirdly sweet, while also horribly intrusive. It shows Griffin cradling me in his arms, his lips pressed gently against my forehead. Then below the photo, an obnoxious headline screams: *Vampires and Billionaires and Bears, Oh My!*

Scrolling down, I read the article.

Tahoe police were in for quite a surprise on Wednesday morning when emergency services responded to a loose bear call at the palatial estate of a local resident.

Officers arrived at the scene to discover the bear was loose *inside* the home of none other than everyone's favorite billionairess, Scarlet Branson, whose company StarReach IPOed last year, sky-rocketing the young female scientist to the top of the list of America's richest women. All before she turned twenty-eight years old.

Fortunately, Ms. Branson made it to the safety of a panic room in her home and was uninjured in the incident. But that's not where the drama ends.

As wildlife rescue officials tranquilized the bear to move him to a safer habitat—away from multimillion-dollar mansions—guess who came running on to the scene like a vampire bat out of hell? None other than Hollywood heart-throb, Griffin Stone.

Famous for his leading role as vampire detective Darius Nightshade on the hit paranormal drama *White Knightshade* and two-time winner of the Hottest Man Alive award, Griffin Stone has long been rumored to have an on-again/off-again relationship with series co-star Mina Harris, who plays Belladonna Westenra. Recently, however, Stone left the Hollywood Hills for his hometown of South Lake Tahoe.

Stone and Branson both attended high school in South Lake Tahoe and were spotted around town together this week, fueling rumors the two have rekindled a long-lost love. If these photos are any indication, we'd say the rumors are true!

Following the article is a collection of photos taken with an impossibly long lens, showing Griffin cradling me against him and kissing my forehead. And me with crazy hair and tears in my eyes looking at him like he hung the moon.

I roll over and shake Griffin awake, holding the phone in

front of his face as he grumbles and blinks his eyes open. Eventually, he reads it and grumbles again, "See, this is why my agent wants me to play a rapist. They called me a vampire. Not a movie star, not an actor, a *vampire*."

"Really? That's your takeaway from the article?"

"What other takeaway is there?"

"That the world thinks we're dating."

"Well, aren't we?"

I freeze, frowning at him. Griffin rolls onto his side and strokes his palm down to my hip. "Scarlet, we had sex four times last night—a personal best—and I plan to increase that exponentially. Do the math, STEM girl; we're dating."

"I guess, sure, but I don't need the details of my sex life broadcast to the world. How am I supposed to command respect from my peers and colleagues when I'm half of a Hollywood couple with some stupid nickname like 'Scarfin' or 'Griflet'?"

He laughs.

"It's not funny."

"It's kind of funny. Scarfin. Heh."

I climb out of the bed to put some distance between myself and Griffin's gorgeous, naked body, his mesmerizing mouth, and sinful touch. Pacing the room, I chew on a fingernail—terrific, now I'm picking up that nasty habit again—and I'm naked.

I go to my closet for my robe and pause at the gashes in the door from the bear attack. That's all this was, right? My life was in peril, and I needed sex to help me feel alive. Griffin was just, well, there. It's not dating. I don't do serious.

But he's *the one*. No. He *was* the one, when I was a girl. Now I'm a woman with other priorities. There is no *one* for me.

And speaking of…I glance at the clock on my phone. I need to leave for the airport soon to make my meeting in San Jose with the board of directors.

"I can't do this right now. I need you to go."

"You can't do what right now?" Griffin sits up, and the sheets pool at his waist as he scowls at me.

"I need you to leave."

"What are you really saying, Scarlet?"

"I…" I can't maintain eye contact. I stare at my feet when I say, "I can't do this."

"Do what? Me? This conversation? What are you saying?"

"Any of this. I can't date a television star. I can't be stalked by celebrity tabloids. I can't have that in my life."

"You mean you can't have *me* in your life."

"It's not you; it's the situation."

"What situation? Afraid to be seen with a washed-up television star?"

"You're not washed up."

He smirks.

"Griffin, I swear, this isn't about you; it's about me."

"Jesus, that line. Really, Scarlet?"

"You don't understand."

He comes off the bed, standing naked before me, his vulnerability clear in his voice. "Then explain it to me."

"Griffin…" I huff, and my shoulders sink as I try to form the right words. "I'm a woman in a male-dominated field. Do you have any idea how hard I've had to work to gain their respect? And now, this young woman at the top of her field is making headlines for dating a vampire heartthrob? What does that do to my credibility as a scientist, as a business leader?"

"Why do you care what they think?"

"My career is important to me." *It's all I have.*

"Do you think it would matter even one iota if any of your colleagues turned up at a cocktail party with an actress on his arm?"

I frown. He's not even listening. "No, it wouldn't matter

because that hypothetical colleague is a *man*. The same rules do not apply."

"So break the rules, Scarlet. You're the queen of your field. Rewrite the goddamn rules." He smirks at me. "But why waste energy fighting the patriarchy over something so meaningless as a fling with a vampire heartthrob."

"Griff—"

My phone rings in my hand. It's my CFO, probably looking to brief me on the high points of the presentation we're going to make to the board in a few hours.

"Answer it. I'm sure it's important," Griffin says and turns his back on me to collect his jeans from the floor.

I let the call go to voice mail as Griffin shoves his legs into his jeans. I need to say or do something to stop him, to make this better, easier for us both. But I don't know what that thing is.

When he's dressed, he turns and stares at me. I expect to find hurt in his expression, but he's donned a mask of indifference. His expression is void of emotion, the actor acting. "Well, it was fun, at least. Good luck with your career, Scarlet."

He turns to leave, and I reach for him. "Wait—"

"For what?" he asks, a hint of his frustration revealed in his tone. Still, he waits, giving me a chance to save this, to save *us*.

My mouth opens and closes, but I remain silent.

"I've waited long enough." And with that, he leaves.

∽

I take a deep breath and roll my shoulders a few times, trying to loosen my tense muscles. At least my hands aren't shaking anymore. *I can do this.*

Pushing through the conference room door, I find the seats around the oval table mostly empty while the members of our board of directors and C-level company executives mingle. The cloying air is rich with expensive cologne, and I swallow the urge to vomit.

A hush falls over the room as the door swings closed behind me. I move toward my seat at the head of the table, halfway there when Marshall Thorn—the least useful, yet most influential member of the board—bellows, "There she is."

He elbows his way toward me, leading with an outstretched hand and giving me his full-wattage salesman smile as he approaches. Out of habit, I accept his hand, and he immediately tightens his grip to pull me closer, furrowing his brow as he stares at my neck. I stumble awkwardly and try to extricate my hand from his as he exclaims, "Doesn't look like he left any bite marks."

To my horror, his little joke elicits a few chuckles from the other men in the room. The only other woman, Margolyn, my chief of marketing, pales as much as I do.

"At least none that I can see," Marshall adds with a wink.

He lets my hand go, and I stumble back a step, staring wide-eyed, absolutely stunned.

After all the bullshit I've endured—gatekeepers trying to block my path, the ice-queen jokes, quid pro quo expectations of male colleagues who helped me along the way—I naively thought I was past it all. Yet, here in this room filled with the top power brokers in the technology field, I've been denigrated to nothing more than the butt of a sex joke.

And the worst part about this moment is Marshall's snide grin. He knows he can get away with this. No one would dare to challenge the mighty Marshall Thorn.

Well, he's wrong about that. Griffin was right. I'm the queen of this field. I make the rules now.

Like a crown has been laid upon my head, I straighten my posture as I continue toward my position at the head of the table, calling the meeting to order. "Shall we begin?"

Marshall moves to a seat at the table along with everyone else, seeming disappointed he didn't get a rise out of me. Colton, my CFO, points the remote at the projector to begin the presentation, but I stand and interrupt, "Before we begin the presentation, I have a few words I'd like to say."

Chairs squeak as everyone turns their attention to my end of the table. I reach into my tote, pulling out my reading material from the flight here, and begin.

"As a reminder to all parties present in this room, I'd like to read a portion of our company's sexual harassment policy." More chairs squeak as some of the men lean back and cross their arms over their chests. Marshall smirks.

I continue. "StarReach defines sexual harassment as 'unwelcome conduct of a sexual nature which makes a person feel offended, humiliated and/or intimidated. This can include situations where a person is asked to engage in sexual activity as a condition of employment, as well as situations which create a hostile, intimidating, or humiliating environment for the recipient.' One of the examples mentioned is 'comments on a worker's appearance, age, private life, etc.' Mr. Thorn, your comment regarding my private life violates this policy."

"Oh, come on Scarlet, it was just a joke."

"Funny you should mention that. The next example given is 'sexual comments, stories, and jokes.'"

"Scarlet, really, you're going to need to grow tougher skin than this if you want to survive in this world."

"Ironically, Mr. Thorn, another example is 'condescending or paternalistic remarks.' You're three for three."

I give him a cold smile, daring him to speak again. When he doesn't, I address the room. "Understand this: my skin is very tough. I've worked hard to be where I am, and I've tolerated quite a lot to get here. My tolerance for harassing behavior ends now. Looking forward, I expect the details of my private life to remain private."

A silence lingers before Henry Wise, always the devil's advocate, says, "To be fair, Ms. Branson, your *private* life is featured on the cover of every gossip magazine in the country today."

"That is accurate, Mr. Wise. As I recall, the details of your second divorce made headlines, too. Yet your personal matters were never addressed in our meetings." Henry's complexion drains of color when I reference the scandalous accusations of infidelity and multi-million-dollar settlement. To the room, I state, "I understand that as CEO of StarReach, my decorum both inside and outside of this office reflects on the company, so in that regard, headlines about my personal life could be a matter of concern for the board. However, nothing in today's article or accompanying photos is in any way inappropriate. As long as my behavior does not harm the reputation of this company, I ask that you refrain from including the topic of my personal life on the meeting agenda."

A few men nod while Margolyn, my sole sister in the room, grins. Marshall, likely stunned by my audacity, gapes. This is, after all, a meeting of the board of directors. These men have the power to fire me.

Well, let them try. I'm sure the fees I'll pay Gloria Allred's firm to litigate my case will fund their pro bono work for years.

With that thought, I clap my hands and start the meeting. "Okay. Let's go over the 10-Q and discuss our first quarter findings."

∾

"Legend-ary!" Margolyn gushes as we settle into the seats around my desk.

"Tell me everything. Leave nothing out," Maria says,

wide-eyed, as she takes the seat beside Margolyn on the other side of my desk.

Margolyn goes into a full retelling of my speech. She even consults notes she took to quote me directly at one point.

"Amazing." Maria beams.

"Sometimes people just need to be reminded when they've crossed a line." I try to sound diplomatic, though I totally feel like a boss bitch right now.

We laugh, and Margolyn leans in closer. "Okay, if you don't want to talk about this, I will never ask again...but, this whole Griffin Stone thing...I mean, *is* it a thing?"

I don't know how to answer that. He is literally the only man I've ever wanted to love from the time I was a teenager, and he's only improved with age. He's kind and thoughtful, creative and hardworking, incredibly fun to be around, and a stallion in the sack. My God, the sex was so good. Yet, I ended things because I was too afraid of what the Marshall Thorns of the world might think.

I open my mouth to speak, but before I can, Maria chimes in, "Griffin Stone says they're just old friends."

I frown at Maria. "He said that?"

She nods.

"When?"

"Uh..." She looks at her phone, scrolling and clicking a few times. "About an hour ago, in an interview with *TMZ*. He says, 'Scarlet and I are old friends from high school. We both happened to be in town at the same time and caught up over dinner a few nights ago. I called her yesterday with a question, and she answered from her safe room, so I went to her house to make sure she was okay. Like any good friend would do.' "

Did he go to the media to dispel the rumors? "Can I see that?"

Maria hands me her phone. I scroll through the interview where Griffin skillfully dodges questions about the show while tamping down the speculation about his relationship with me. I hug Maria's phone to my chest, and she and Margolyn frown at me.

"Oh no, Scarlet, did you want it to be more with Griffin?" Margolyn asks.

"It is more." I hand Maria's phone back, then stand and pace behind my desk, trying to understand why Griffin would do something so selfless for the woman who basically broke his heart...again. Mostly to myself, I mutter, "I can't believe he did this."

"I'm so sorry, Scarlet," Maria says. She and Margolyn both look sympathetic.

Margolyn adds, "What a horrible way to break up with someone."

I stop my pacing and, to Maria, I say, "Have my pilot prepare a flight plan for Tahoe."

"But...you're attending the museum gala tonight."

"Send my regrets. I need to see Griffin."

"Scarlet." Margolyn stands and approaches me like a friend about to offer comfort. "Are you sure you should go to him right now? After he hurt you like this? Maybe take a minute to—"

"That wasn't a breakup. That was Griffin sacrificing himself for me. But he doesn't need to. Stupidly, I convinced him I would let men like Marshall control me. But I won't. I will date Griffin Stone, and there's nothing they can do about it."

"So, you are dating him?" both women ask.

"Yes! I am dating Griffin Stone!" I proclaim as I bundle my laptop and other belongings into my tote bag. "Now, I just need to go inform him of that fact."

## CHAPTER 16
*Griffin*

"What's the matter with you?" Tricia asks as she dumps a basket of laundry on my lap. "You ran out of here like your tush was on fire. Didn't come home until the next day. And now it's like my couch grew a tumor shaped an awful lot like my baby brother."

"Tush?" I raise an eyebrow at my sister. She eyes her boys pointedly, silently reminding me we don't say words like "butt" or "ass" in front of them unless we want to hear them sing that word on repeat for the next forty-eight hours. It's not like they'd notice; they're in the middle of a game that requires them to holler and chase each other in circles. Where do kids get their boundless energy? And how do I make it stop?

Tricia plops down beside me, and we both fold the laundry and stack it on the coffee table. "Is this about your job again?"

Actually, no. For once, I'm not mourning the loss of my youth and career. I shrug, though, because I don't want to talk about my sour mood.

"Or maybe it's about Scarlet?" Damn. My sister is too observant. I always hated that about her. She watches me from the corner of her eye and must notice me wince at the sound of Scarlet's name. "Oh my God, it's true?"

"What's true?"

"You're dating Scabby Scar?"

"Don't call her that. And don't believe everything you read on the internet."

Ignoring me, she goes on. "She used to have such a big crush on you. It was adorable."

"What?" I frown at her. "You could tell?"

"Oh, Little Grifter, everyone could see it. She was always so together, especially for a kid. She had everything figured out, except around you. She'd get so tongue tied and googly eyed. You made a mess out of her."

"She made a mess out of me."

My sister squeezes my shoulder. "Okay, so spill it. What happened?"

How do I even begin to explain the complex combination of emotions I feel for Scarlet and the roller coaster of these last few days? *Well, I fell back in love. She didn't.* I guess it's not as complex as I thought. I hollowed myself out and gave every part of my heart to Scarlet. Then she left and took all of me with her.

Before I can formulate a response, someone pounds on the front door. All three of Tricia's demon spawn race toward it.

"What did I say, boys? Don't answer the door without an adult present," Tricia shouts as she eyes me. I guess I'm supposed to be the present adult.

Walking to the door feels like trudging through mud. I arrive as Tricia's middle son, Bowen, swings the door open to Rob, as well as Paula and Julie. *What the hell?*

"You ready?" Rob asks.

"Ready for what?"

"Karaoke night at The Silver Lining, duh. Come on, dude."

I hate karaoke. Okay, that's not true. I used to like karaoke.

Now if I perform, I risk landing on YouTube with a thousand comments proposing marriage or nitpicking my singing. What's the point of going to karaoke if I can't perform?

I reach for an excuse, finding three of them standing around me, quickly growing bored with this conversation. "I'm going to stay here, help my sister with the boys—"

I nearly jump out of my skin when Tricia chimes in from my side. "Actually, Little Grifter, the boys are having a sleepover with their friend Stephen tonight, and I love karaoke!"

The boys all burst into spontaneous cheers and run to their rooms to prepare for their sleepover. Paula and Julie clap and hoot, too.

Fine. I go to my room to change out of my *White Knightshade* Season five crew party tee shirt and into something more socially appropriate before leaving with Rob and the ladies, while Tricia takes the boys over to their friend's house. Within half an hour, we've reconvened around a high-top table between the bar and the stage at The Silver Lining.

With a drink in my hand and a smile on my face, I just want to have fun with my friends and family. I can make that happen. I'm a pretty decent actor.

Gayle Weathers, one of the Silver Lining's owners—a group of divorcees who pooled their money to buy this place a decade ago—is hosting tonight. Each of the owners has her own karaoke playlist, so the mood of the night depends on the hostess. Gayle is big on Abba. She's also a *Buffy* fan—Gayle was the wise elder/neighborhood babysitter who turned a young and impressionable Scarlet on to the show all those years ago—and has the *Buffy* musical songs on her playlist.

It only takes one of the bar's signature Rum Runner cocktails for me to consider singing Spike's song. And after my second drink, I'm signing up as the list gets passed to our table. Gayle gives me a hell of an introduction before I walk up onto that short stage, clutch the microphone like a punk rocker, and transform into the heartbroken vampire.

I can practically hear my agent's eyes roll in his head at my seemingly pathological need to be typecast as a damned vampire. But this isn't Hollywood; it's Tahoe between the seasons. Without all the tourists here for the winter or summer seasons, the crowd at The Silver Lining is mostly regulars, people I've known all my life. Here, I'm not some stupid television vampire. I'm Little Grifter, Tony and Pat's son, Tricia's brother. Here, I'm accepted for being me. So I belt out the lyrics about pain and rejection without fear of notoriety. Then I get another drink from the bartender.

I'm three cocktails to the wind when Gayle announces, "We have a special guest tonight, an old friend of these parts. Give a warm welcome to Scarlet Branson, everyone."

*Wait. What?*

I sit up a little straighter and focus on the stage as the woman of my dreams steps up to the microphone and looks out at the crowd like she's searching for someone. When her eyes meet mine, she leans close to the microphone and says, "I'd like to—"

The microphone squeals with feedback. Scarlet winces and takes a step back, giving the thing some space.

"Sorry," she murmurs. Then she says it again, once more with feeling. "I'm sorry. I'm so sorry. I was afraid and I let that fear rule me. But you're right, Griffin, I'm the queen now. I rule and I make the rules. I'm not going to let anyone stop me from falling in love with you."

Were it not for the gasp heard 'round the room, I'd think I was imagining this. Did she say…?

"So I have a question for you, Griffin," Scarlet says into the mic, then nods to Gayle, who's manning the DJ booth. She focuses her next words into the microphone, and her voice shakes a little as she sings, "Where Do We Go from Here?" from the *Buffy* musical. My God, it's so sweet and romantic.

In an instant, I'm out of my seat, weaving between the tables that separate me from the stage. By now, Gayle has her own microphone, and she's singing the Giles part as she leads the rest of the room to sing as well—this is an ensemble piece anyway. Accepting my role as Spike, I step up onto the stage and pull Scarlet away from the microphone to wrap her in my arms.

"I'm so sorry, Griffin," she whispers against my neck. "Can you forgive me?"

"Already did," I say and plant a claiming kiss on her lips. The room roars with applause. Scarlet and I come apart to catch our breath and look out at our audience. Everyone is singing, and Rob is swaying a lighter through the air.

"Holy shit. Did you plan this?"

Scarlet bites her lip and nods.

"Even my sister was in on it?"

Scarlet smiles.

"Jesus, that's theatrical. And really romantic." I squeeze her against me and bury my nose in her hair, breathing in my favorite scent. I pull away to ask, "I'm a little drunk, Scarlet, so I need you to clarify: are we dating?"

"Yes." She giggles, then turns to the microphone to loudly proclaim, "We're dating."

With that, I pull her back into my arms and kiss her while everyone sings the part about how the curtains close on a kiss.

## CHAPTER 17

*Griffin*

### Two Weeks Later

The call comes just before dawn. Darius only has minutes to reach the warehouse and save his beloved Belladonna before the sun will rise on them both. He races with such paranormal speed, the humans he passes on the sidewalk only notice a slight breeze as he blows by on his way to the industrial park that stretches along the western shore of Lake Michigan.

The area is a known haunt for the local werewolf pack, led by Lucius. But Darius is panicked and doesn't think to call McLintoch or Henri for backup. As he reaches the gates to the industrial complex, he smells them, werewolves, lots of them, and on a night when the moon is full.

He knows this is a fool's errand the moment he steps into the dark warehouse. The only light is a shaft of moonlight, which spills into the room through the shattered panes of the high windows on the brick walls.

"Well, well, well, I didn't actually expect you to show up," Lucius says, looking smug as a cadre of warrior werewolves step out of the shadows, flanking Darius and surrounding him.

"Where is she?"

"Safe and sound in my bed, carrying my child."

"You lie."

"Do I?"

Lucius takes a step closer, circling. Darius circles, too, keeping an eye on his chief rival as he tries to track the movements of the wolf pack around him. More come out of the shadows, howling and growling, forming a perfect circle around the moonlit spot where Darius and Lucius face off.

One of the werewolves swipes at Darius, forcing him toward Lucius, who takes his own shot. But his claws catch only air as Darius bends low and leaps high, reaching as he springs into the air and comes to rest in a crouch on one of the rafters over their heads.

From his vantage point, he sees hundreds of werewolves, with more pouring into the warehouse from the docks. Darius looks to the windows as an escape. If he can reach them, he can run across the roofs of the nearby buildings, and he might have a chance. But the distance to the windows is too far.

From below, Lucius yells, "She has outgrown you, Darius. You do not have what she needs now. We do. She has accepted her fate. She will be my queen and bear my heir. The prophesied hybrid will be born of our union to rule over us all."

"Fairy tales! Fantasy! Belladonna would never betray her kind. Your dreams are born of ashes, and you will burn with them," Darius says as he balances on the rafter, looking for a route to the window. But some of the wolves are climbing the walls to reach his beam as they close in on his position from both sides.

"The only ash here is you, Darius," Lucius jokes, and the wolves laugh. But he's right. Darius can sense the approaching dawn. Time is running out. Looking to the wolves leaping toward him from both sides, he crouches and jumps.

He stretches as far as he can, reaching with everything inside him, pulling from the strength of his proud vampire ancestors, and lands hard against the brick wall, one hand grasping the edge of a window.

Jagged bits of broken glass cut into Darius's palm as he pulls himself up to the edge of the window. But outside, another werewolf waits for him on the roof. This one is in full wolf form, and she looks different from the rest. Where their coats are dark, her white fur glitters in the moonlight.

Darius recognizes her before she shifts, his heart breaking as the pearlescent fur stretches and morphs into Belladonna's long white hair when she transitions back to her vampire form.

Her onyx eyes glisten with unshed tears, and she gives him a pitying look. "I'm sorry, Darius, but this is who I am now. You're too set in your ways to comprehend the future that awaits. A great change is coming, and there is nothing you can do to stop it."

Belladonna crouches before him and strokes Darius's hand, touching him gently, even as the window glass cuts through his skin. One tear tracks down her ivory cheek. "I loved you once."

"I will always love you," Darius says to her.

"I know, and that's the problem. I didn't want to hurt you, dear Darius, but you've left me no choice." With those parting words, she pushes him off the window ledge.

Darius's expression changes from surprise to devastating betrayal as he reaches for her and grasps only air, falling in slow motion to the ground and the pack of ravenous wolves below. He lands in a maelstrom of raking claws and snapping jaws, disappearing into the chaos as the wolves descend and tear him to shreds.

"What the actual *fuck*?" Julie jumps up, spilling popcorn all over the floor as she screams at Scarlet's television.

I laugh as the entire room erupts in outrage, watching the gore with increasing horror as they realize there's no coming back from that. The writers can't bring back a disassembled vampire, it's just not done.

"Seriously, dude." Rob turns to me. "Did you just die?"

"I did. I am officially unemployed!" I beam, feeling surprisingly light and happy about the whole situation.

"Thank God I don't have to keep that secret anymore," my sister hollers from her seat on the couch and downs the rest of her cocktail.

"You knew?" Paula and Julie turn on her, as if she's betrayed them.

I'm having a blast watching them freak out and imagining the millions of fans screaming at their televisions right now. If I'm going to retire from television, I might as well go out in a blaze of glory. And that scene was a glorious goddamn blaze.

But Scarlet's reaction is my favorite. She wraps her arms around me and kisses me like she's watched the hottest porno and wants to try out the moves with me.

"That vampire growl you made when one of the werewolves tore your arm off was sexy, Griff," she says against my neck. I hike her up onto the kitchen counter and nibble at her neck as I growl again, just for her. She spikes her nails through my hair and pulls me to her for a deep kiss.

I should have known a werewolf blood orgy would do the trick with Scarlet. My baby's a little bit freaky, and I like it.

"Get a room, you two," Rob grumbles as he angles past us to grab another beer from the fridge.

"My thoughts exactly," I answer as I pick Scarlet up from the counter and carry her to her bedroom.

Scarlet hollers over my shoulder to our guests. "Stay as long as you want. Help yourself to food and drink and let yourselves out. Night y'all."

"Are they going to bone?" Paula asks.

"Duh," Julie says.

"Gross. Stop talking about my baby brother boning," my sister shouts.

I kick Scarlet's bedroom door closed and toss her onto the bed. She manages to strip out of her clothes in seconds, and I'm hopping on one foot as I struggle to do the same. When I finally get my boots off and my jeans with them, I take a breath and come down beside Scarlet on the bed. She rolls me onto my back with a kiss and comes up, straddling me.

She skips right past the foreplay and comes down on my cock with a sexy gasp. Fuck, she's dripping wet, and it turns me on that watching me massacred on television gets her so excited. Slowly, she fucks me, shifting her hips forward and back until she's driving me wild with her subtle movements and the way she arches her back and stretches her arms over her head. She pulls her hair up onto her head, then lets it go in a red cascade down her back as she rides me to her sweet ecstasy.

"Fuck," I mumble as she collapses across my chest. I take her in my arms and roll until she's under me and I can drive deep inside her, prolonging her orgasm as I chase my own.

I come with a gasp and a groan, and I collapse, too. We turn onto our sides, still smiling, as I push her hair out of her face.

"I died today, Scarlet."

"I saw."

"I died and I went to heaven."

Scarlet's smile widens.

"Is it too soon to say I love you?" I ask her, whispering the words, almost like I'm afraid for her to hear.

She pulls me close, brushing an excruciatingly soft kiss across my lips. "It's not too soon, and it's not too late either. I love you, too. I always have. I always will."

∼

If you enjoyed *Wishing Upon a Star*, you'll love *Hearts on Fire*. Keep reading for a preview as firefighter cat dad Drew and his sexy new neighbor Chloe are brought together by Drew's ornery three-legged cat.

## Hearts of Texas Series
PREVIEW

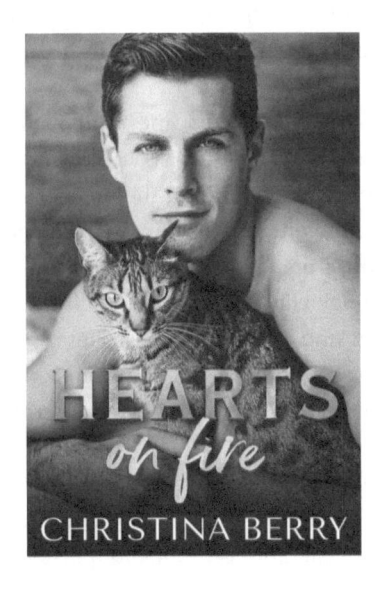

## CHAPTER 1 - CHLOE

"Hey, guy, what part of 'stop peeing on my porch' is unclear?"

The asshole blinks at me like he doesn't understand.

Which, of course, he doesn't; he's a cat. I mean, he's a cute cat—a beautiful brown tabby with gorgeous green eyes, a missing leg, and a bobbed tail that wiggles adorably when he pisses on my porch. Nonetheless, he's pissing on my porch, which pisses me off.

"Are you marking your territory? Cuz, this is *my* territory now, buddy."

He—I don't know for certain he is a 'he,' but any animal that pees all over a stranger's porch must be male—cocks his head to the side, gives me a long-suffering stare, crosses to a different corner of the porch, and pees there too.

*Dick.*

Too tired to care, I roll my eyes at the pissy visitor and drop my ass with a harrumph to the top step of the porch stairs. Overheated, I fan my face while I guzzle a bottle of water.

The yard is a rocky landscape with feathery plumes of savannah grass, spiky rosettes of yucca, and long, lavender fingers of purple sage waving in the breeze, and I marvel yet again at how different this terrain is from the other side of Austin. My house on the east side of town has a lush green yard made of thick clay soil, covered with ivy, and shaded by towering pecan and sycamore trees. Here, only thirty miles west, the topsoil barely covers the limestone bedrock, and nothing but mesquite, persimmon, and scrubby clumps of live oak take root.

At least the heat here is drier. After a morning spent tearing down the rotted ceiling of my living room, I'm coated in a layer of sweat and century-old plaster dust, and I'm thankful for the shade and breeze the wraparound porch provides.

I hold the still-chilled bottle of water against my temple and finally start to feel refreshed but jump about a foot in the air with the tickle of whiskers against my arm. The cat jumps, too, his back arches, and his stumpy tail poofs out about three times its original size.

"Whoa there, buddy. Warn a girl before you rub up on her."

The cat blinks at me and deflates from his defensive stance, meowing like we're having a nice chat.

"We're friends now, are we? You're a fickle little pisser, aren't you?"

He meows again, and I hold out my hand for his inspection before I try to pet him. He gives my fingers a sniff and crinkles his nose at my stink.

"I know, right? Whose genius idea was it to renovate this house in August?" It's got to be one hundred and five degrees today, *in the shade*. And inside the house—even with all the windows open and a box fan spinning at top speed—the heat index is surely pushing triple-digit teens.

The porch pisser shares a bit of his cat wisdom with me and flops down onto the dusty old floorboards, glancing over his shoulder, expecting attention. I give it.

With a few pets, he transforms from standoffish to a lusty love monster. Like a demon possessed, he flops to-and-fro, scoots hither and thither, and meows madly, demanding affection.

"Wow, dude, you're kind of intense."

The cat gets back on his feet, his dark-striped coat now dusty and covered with bits of leaves and cobwebs. He meows loudly and headbutts my arm in response.

"What's your name?" He's not wearing a tag, but—despite his dirt bath—he looks clean, cared for, and well-fed. Plus, he's way too friendly to be a stray. Someone, somewhere loves this guy. "You lost?"

This close, I have a better view of his back end. With his stubby tail and missing left hind leg, it's clear he suffered a terrible injury, but he walks almost as well as a four-legged cat. "What happened, buddy? You get hurt?"

He meows, and I'm starting to like this guy. He is my type, after all: a beautiful, scarred boy who pisses all over everything.

"Well, it was nice meeting you, but I have to get back to work." I give the cat a couple more heavy pets as I rise to my feet, wipe the dust off my ass, and head toward the door.

The cat meows and tangles himself around my legs a few times. I take a last deep breath of the fresh air before putting my respirator and goggles back on. With a goodbye wave, I close the door in the cat's face and return my focus to the renovation project.

∾

The Krause house is old, as in one-of-the-first-German-settlements-during-the-early-days-of-Texas-statehood old, and once upon a time it was the only house up on this dusty hill. But over the years, the land was subdivided and developed into a comfortable country neighborhood. Now, this old house is just one of a dozen acreages dotting Lazy River Road.

The neighborhood is a strange blend of suburban sprawl meets rural backwoods. Some properties are ringed by ranch-rail fences with electronic gates and concrete driveways that curve around scrawny oaks and manicured agave toward big brick McMansions. Less prosperous neighbors line their land with barbed wire, and gravel drives angle past evergreen thickets of Ashe juniper shrubs toward double-wides set on cinder block.

Rich or poor, though, none of the houses fit in here. The signs and symptoms of humanity look out of place in this rugged land.

Despite its age, the Krause house is no exception. The bright white Folk Victorian farmhouse hardly blends with its rocky surroundings. Inside, the misfit nature of the house continues. Turning my aspiring-architect eye to the details, I glance around the empty rooms of my family's legacy, always so fascinated by the blend of styles.

Over the years, each generation of Krause updated and expanded the house. Only the wide plank floors remain from the original dogtrot farmhouse. The breezeway was enclosed after the Civil War. Near the turn of the twentieth century, the porch was outfitted with all sorts of gingerbread detail. In the living room, the far wall was outfitted at some point with ornate Craftsman-style woodwork and built-in curios flanking the fireplace. There's crown molding around the ceilings, too, which were raised several feet when electricity was installed. The back of the house was extended when plumbing came in. And it was weather tightened when air-conditioning was added.

And it's that air conditioner that is the bane of my existence. While I would love to spend time imagining what architectural detail I'll add to the blend of family history, it seems my generation has been left to clean up the mess my family left behind. In this case, an antique air conditioner that flooded the living room ceiling.

Removing rotten drywall and ancient plaster off the ceiling of a twelve-foot-tall room when all you have is a pry bar and an eight-foot ladder is challenging. Within an hour, I'm coated with a second layer of dust, itching all over, and about to succumb to heat exhaustion.

Out on the porch for another water break, I find the cat still there. He meows loudly and weaves between my ankles until I give up trying to walk and plop down on the doormat. I tear the respirator and goggles off my face and take a deep breath of the fresh air. The cat climbs up my arm, pawing at me—not asking for attention but demanding it.

"Jeez, dude, chill." I take a deep drink of water before I start to pet the needy guy. If there was any doubt, it's clear the cat isn't a stray. He's spoiled rotten.

I glance up and down Lazy River Road, a narrow two-lane with more bends than its namesake, but everything is spread out, and the only place I can see from my porch is Inez's house next door.

Getting an idea, I chug the rest of my water then pull my phone out and snap a few photos of the cat sprawled like a Playgirl centerfold across my porch. I compose a quick message—"Who's cat is this?"—and attach a couple of the images, then text them to Inez.

Inez Rodriguez—devoted widow to Emmanuel, mother of three, and grandmother of twelve—brought over with a tin of her homemade pecan pralines the first morning I moved in.

She'd managed to tell me her life story and the full history of her Tejano family back to the days before the Alamo, then programmed her number into my phone within the first fifteen minutes of knowing her. She's the best next-door neighbor I've ever had, and already, three days later, I've found my first occasion to reach out.

I startle when Inez says, "¡Hola! ¡Buenas tardes!"

The little woman steps through a gap between her climbing roses—our properties are among the few around here without fences—and waves. She's beautiful, with straight silvery hair cut in a bob at her chin, bright curious eyes, and deep laugh lines bracketing her smile, evidence of a life filled with happiness.

I push to stand, dusting off my hands and backside. Compared to her colorful, embroidered blouse and cornflower capri pants, I feel woefully underdressed and rather gross in my shorts and tank top, coated in sweat and dirt.

I respond, "¡Hola, Inez!" as she crosses the yard to meet me in the shade of the porch.

"I see you've met Bodhi," she says as the cat goes to her, and she gives him a scratch under the chin. She's a tiny woman and barely has to stoop to reach him.

A quick glance at the barren state of my porch reminds me

of what a terrible hostess I am. Such a gorgeous wraparound, well adorned with whimsical, gingerbread trim, and not a chair in sight. I can't offer my neighbor a seat.

Inez doesn't seem to mind, contentedly crouched as she babies the cat. "He must have slipped his noose again."

"His noose?"

Inez grins at me. "His collars. He's always losing them."

"Is Bodhi your cat?"

"Oh no, he's Drew's baby."

"Who's Drew?"

"This little devil's daddy."

*Daddy?*

"He lives in Ricky's house." Inez points in the general direction of her own house.

I scan through my memory of that first data-dump conversation I had with Inez. Ricky is the youngest of her three sons. He lived in the house next door to Inez until a few years ago, when he moved to San Antonio.

Okay. I nod with more certainty now and deposit two new names into my memory bank—Bodhi the cat and his daddy, Drew.

"Nothing but trouble."

"Trouble?"

My mind flashes to all the crime documentaries I've seen about small-town Texas trouble—meth-lab chemists, racist Klansmen, weird family disputes that stretch as far back as Sam Houston's Lone Star Presidency—so I laugh when she shakes her head and her expression goes grave. "Too good-looking, just like this handsome man. He's irresistible, and he knows it. Nothing but trouble."

Her serious expression cracks wide with a smile, and she waggles her brows suggestively as she flicks the stump of Bodhi's missing tail. He purrs and meows for more, and my heart melts. Totally irresistible. Nothing but trouble, indeed.

"What happened to him?" I ask about Bodhi's missing leg and tail.

"Fire," Inez answers and shifts on her feet like she's uncomfortable. Is it the topic or lack of seating causing her discomfort? I change the subject from one to the other. "Inez, would you like to sit down? I can grab the stool from the kitchen and make us some tea."

"Oh no, *cariño*, don't trouble yourself. If I sit, I might not get up again. I was heading down to visit Al at the hardware co-op and saw your message. Thought I'd stop by for a quick visit. Thanks for keeping an eye on this boy while his daddy's away," she says as she turns and leaves, waving when she reaches the end of my drive.

"Okay, well, bye then," I say to myself and glance down at Bodhi. He's lying on his back, his three legs splayed, shameless and purring loudly. "Where's your daddy?"

Bodhi answers me, but I don't understand.

"You know, I don't remember volunteering for this cat-sitting job." I frown at him. "You turn up and pee on my porch, and now I'm responsible for you? Not cool."

He ignores me, intensely focused on grooming his genitals. The layer of dust coating my skin itches. It's time for me to clean myself as well. I leave Bodhi to his bath and go inside for my own.

## CHAPTER 2 - CHLOE

Pinned beneath the unbearable weight of the car, I can't move. The pain in my arm is excruciating. My nostrils fill with the acrid stench of smoke. Strobes of red and blue lights glitter in the broken glass. Dizziness and panic twist together in my belly, turning sour like sickness.

Except... *Wait*. This isn't real. It's the nightmare. My brain's playing her stupid games again. In the hazy place between wakefulness and sleep, I try to remember the coping exercises my therapist, Erica, taught me.

"Wiggle your toes and fingers," she says in my mind, her soothing voice centering me as I do what she instructs to push myself through the sleep paralysis. "Take a deep breath in and out."

But something's different this time. Something's...purring, and the weight bearing down on my chest moves; it steps on my left tit.

"Ouch!" I yelp and bolt upright. A cat tumbles onto the sheets beside me.

I roll off my mattress and almost kick over the lamp on the floor as I try to turn it on. When there's light, I find Bodhi in my bed.

"What in the hell? How did you get in here?"

Still groggy and confused, I rub my sore boob as I glance around the room, finally noticing the opening in my window. I'd stuffed a piece of rigid insulated foam into the gap beside my window-unit air conditioner a few days ago when I'd installed it. Now the foam is on the floor, leaving my bedroom open to the outside world.

"Wow, so you're a porch-pissing home invader! Inez is right—you're nothing but trouble."

Bodhi blinks at me. I glance out the opening in the window; it's at least a three-foot drop to the ground from the windowsill.

"Pretty spry for a tripod, I have to admit." I look back at the cat, who's settling comfortably in my sheets. "Oh no you don't. This isn't your house. You need to leave!"

He angles those beautiful green eyes at me as he snuggles deeper into my sheets, looking small and vulnerable in my bed. I glance again out the window at the dark night. What's out there roaming the Texas Hill Country at this hour? Coyotes? Mountain lions? I imagine all manner of monster poised outside my window, waiting to gobble up this poor, little three-legged tabby cat.

"Okay. Fine," I huff. "You can stay tonight. But that's it. You got me?"

I stuff the foam block back into the window beside the air conditioner and click off the light. Returning to bed, I nestle beneath the sheets while Bodhi curls into a ball beside me, purring loudly. The vibration relaxes me.

"I don't take kindly to men manipulating me to get into my bed," I tell him as I pet him.

He headbutts my chest softly, then tucks his head beneath my chin, and I'm putty in his paws.

∼

It's too early. The orange light of the rising sun cuts through the darkness of my bedroom and serves as another reminder I need window coverings in here.

I stir slowly, feeling such peace this morning. It's the cat. Bodhi is curled up against me, so soft and sweet. He purrs in response and does a big stretch, then blinks his beautiful eyes open.

"Good morning, handsome. I'll bet your daddy misses you." Bodhi gives me one of those cute little chirpy meows and rolls over to go back to sleep. "Oh no you don't. Time for you to go home, buddy."

Bodhi is either too tired or enjoys the affection too much to protest as I pick him up and carry him out of my bedroom, up the long hallway, and out to the porch.

Setting him down by the steps, I hustle back into the house before he can dart past me and shut the door in his face. Bodhi stares up at me through the glass portion of the door, looking betrayed.

I explain through the glass, "You don't live here. Go away now, okay?"

The strangeness of this situation warrants an eye roll. "What the hell am I doing? I'm talking to a cat. And now I'm talking to myself about talking to a cat. I need coffee."

In the kitchen, I dig into a box of breakfast bars as I brew some coffee. When I'm fed and awake, I don my work clothes and protective gear, grab the pry bar, climb the ladder—which is still set beneath the massive mess of rotted wood and drywall drooping from the living room ceiling—and get back to demolition work.

A couple hours of toil later, I stand under the hole in the ceiling, wiping the sweat from my brow and trying to catch my breath through the respirator. My muscles are screaming from my work, yet I can barely see the progress I've made. I need a sledgehammer, bigger arms, and a crew of people to help.

Really, what I need is a break and a trip to the hardware co-op. Setting my goggles and respirator by the door, I consider a shower. I'm coated in sweat and drywall dust like I've been tarred and feathered, but I'm sure it's nothing Al at the hardware co-op hasn't seen before. I opt out of the shower and go to the bedroom for my purse.

"What the hell?" That's all I can articulate when I find Bodhi curled on my bed, the block of foam discarded on the floor again. I don't mind the cat so much, but every time he knocks that block of foam out of the window, he invites all sorts of country critters inside. There are scorpions and tarantulas in this part of Texas, and I do not appreciate having to worry about creepy-crawlies in my bed.

"Stop it. This is not okay."

Bodhi doesn't listen. He stretches across the rumpled sheets. I fit the foam back in place, grab the cat and my purse, and head out the front door.

Outside, I deposit Bodhi onto one of the big limestone boulders beside the driveway, then hop in my car and go. As I back out, the cat narrows his eyes at me, plotting. I narrow my eyes, too, plotting back.

∼

At the hardware co-op, I sling an eight-pound sledgehammer over my shoulder and head to the home decor section for some bedroom curtains. In Lawn and Garden, I find a roll of chicken wire to use for keeping uninvited cats out of my bedroom. As I make my way to the register, I pass the pet aisle and stop. There at the end, shining beneath the overhead fluorescent lights, is an engraver machine and beside it a whole assortment of collars and tags.

I consider Bodhi, collarless and wandering the great outdoors. What if he tries to break into someone else's house, and they think he's a stray and take him to the pound? I'm pretty sure the animal shelter out here in the county is a kill shelter, unlike the no-kill Austin shelter. If Bodhi got busted and euthanized because I was too selfish to share my bed, the guilt would crush me.

Which is absurd; he's someone else's cat. I shouldn't be sharing my bed with other people's cats. At least if I get him a collar, no one will mistake him for a stray.

Browsing the collection of collars and tags, I find the perfect set. The collar is bright orange with a jingle bell, and the tag is a matching orange bow tie. It's dapper and daring, and the orange will complement his green eyes. Bodhi will be an icon of country cat fashion.

∼

At home, I dump my new work tools on the living room floor then move to my bedroom where, sure enough, the cat is back.

"Hey, you little porch-pissing home invader, I got you a present."

Bodhi responds to the gentle tone of my voice, trotting to the corner of my bed to meow sweetly at me. I scratch his ears, giving him all my love right before I snap the collar around his neck.

To say he dislikes it is an understatement. The moment the collar closes, Bodhi freaks out. He hisses and claws at the thing. He tears circles across the hardwood floor, trying to outrun it. But where he goes, it goes, and the bell jingles delightfully along with him.

When he calms a bit, he stares daggers at me from the corner, his back arched and stubby tail puffed. He's telegraphing his emotions: We're not friends anymore. I've betrayed him.

But, hey, I didn't ask for him to pee on my porch. I didn't invite him to break into my bedroom repeatedly, letting all the cold air out of the only habitable room in the whole house.

I'm mad too, I remind myself, as I shove the foam back into the open window and nail the chicken wire to the sill so it can't be pushed aside again. When that's done, I open the bedroom door and Bodhi races out. He comes to a screeching halt at the front door, irritably waiting for me to let him outside.

When I do, he rockets across the porch in a few leaping bounds, moving impressively fast for a cat with a missing leg. He jumps to the ground, darting toward the road through the dry prairie grass, cactus, and cockleburs.

That's when I see the truck. It's a big, black pickup I've seen before, always driving too fast on Lazy River Road. I panic as Bodhi aims right for the tires. *Oh God, please don't let me kill that stupid cat over a collar!* But the truck passes without incident, and Bodhi runs after it like a dog chasing cars.

I close my eyes with relief, breathe easier, and shut the door. Excitement over, I don my gloves, goggles, and respirator mask and get back to work. With my new sledgehammer, I perform a good under swing and bring it up to smash against the ceiling. Everything in the house rattles, big chunks of drywall crash to the floor, and dust rains supreme.

## CHAPTER 3 - DREW

I pull into my drive, nursing fantasies of my bed and the hours of sleep I desperately need, when Bodhi jumps through the window of my truck and starts cussing up a storm. Little man is big mad about something, and he's making a dainty jingling sound as he paces across my lap and the seat beside me, telling me about his day. He stops his caterwauling long enough for me to get a good look at the orange collar around his neck.

*The fuck is this shit?* My cat's collar is not orange. It's never been orange, and it will never be orange. It's black, and it doesn't have a jingle bell on it or a cutesy little bow tie tag that sure as shit doesn't say "BS" on it.

"BS? Who the fuck tagged you BS?"

Bodhi bitches some more. I pick him up and carry him over to Inez's house. This seems like something she'd do. And if she didn't, she'll know who did.

Little man squirms in my arms, and that stupid bell tinkles, doing more to emasculate Bodhi than getting him neutered did. Inez looks like she's struggling to keep a straight face as I near her. I narrow my eyes at the little old granny, and she bursts into laughter.

"Bodhito, look how handsome you are in a bow tie."

"Did you do this?"

"Oh no." She laughs again. "Must have been Chloe. Bodhi's taken a shine to her."

"Chloe?" *Who the fuck is Chloe?*

At the sound of this Chloe person's name, Bodhi squirms

again, jingling like a Christmas elf. I don't dare let him go, though, not with some crazy cat tagger lurking around.

"Chloe Krause, Hazel's granddaughter."

"Hazel had a granddaughter?"

"Yes. She's a sweet little thing. She's moved in to renovate the old house."

*What the fuck?* That was going to be my house. Hazel's son, Denny, all but promised to sell it to me when I'd found the guy packing up his mother's belongings shortly after her hospitalization last spring.

I try not to scowl at Inez, the unwitting bearer of this bad news. With a curt nod, I cross through her yard to the Krause property.

I liked Hazel Krause and her house on the hill. I'd help her sometimes when she needed a hand. She always feed me afterward, and we'd sit and watch the sun set over the Hill Country from her porch. Then Hazel got sick last year, and while she spent her last months in hospice, her house sat empty, falling into disrepair as it languished.

I had my sights set on fixing the old place up. It would've been hard work, but that was the appeal, a project. I'd imagined long days of labor followed by lazy evenings watching the sun set from a rocking chair. Disappointment tastes rotten on my tongue, and I try to swallow it away as I take the three creaky steps up onto the porch and aim for the front door.

I go to knock but freeze when I hear music playing inside. It's loud. It's good. It's Rage Against the Machine's "Sleep Now in the Fire," a personal favorite. I smile to myself, charmed by this Chloe woman's taste in music.

In sync with the powerful kick of the drums, a tremendous banging comes from inside the house. Each time this extra wallop hits, the whole building trembles like it's taking a beating with a wrecking ball.

*What the fuck?*

I frown at Bodhi, still clutched in my arm. He frowns back

at me. Curious, I cup my eyes and peer through the window in the door. Off to the left, in the center of the living room, a woman balances on a ladder, swinging a sledgehammer at the ceiling. With each stroke, the house rains dust and bits of shattered ceiling all around her.

*Is she trying to bring down the whole house with herself in the middle of it?*

The instant the song quiets a bit, I pound on the door. My interruption startles her and throws off her rhythm. The sledgehammer swings wide, and the change in momentum nearly pulls her off the ladder.

*Shit!* I almost burst through the door like I plan to catch her if she falls. But she manages to steady herself and descend the ladder with the sledgehammer slung over her shoulder like a badass looking for trouble.

*Hot.*

She approaches, swings the door open, and... She's tiny. Barely above five feet tall, she stares up at me in a pair of too large safety goggles that give her a bug-eyed look. The P100 half-mask respirator is smart lung protection considering the dust she's stirring up, but it's adjusted so high on her nose her goggles fog up every time she exhales.

*Cute.*

Her protective gear ends with nothing more than a pair of leather gloves and bulky steel-toe boots. Her legs and arms are exposed in a tank top and tiny shorts, every inch of her coated with a dusty sheen of sweat.

*Hot again.*

With a harrumph, she sets the sledgehammer on the floor beside the door and pulls the respirator down below her chin. It leaves angry red marks and outlines where the grime on her cheeks meets the edges. She pushes the foggy goggles up onto her head, tangling them in her dark, dusty hair.

Her big brown eyes captivate my attention. I'm stunned

stupid, standing there like an idiot staring at her. She furrows her brow. "Can I help you?"

Oh. Right. I look down at Bodhi in my arms, the orange bow-tie tag reminding me why I came here. I point at it. "What is this?"

"A cat," she answers, looking at me like I'm the asshole here.

"Very fucking funny. I know it's a cat. It's *my* cat, and he's wearing *your* tag. You put a tag on *my* fucking cat. Who do you think you are claiming things that aren't yours?"

"Claiming?"

"Yeah, claiming. That's what a tag is. Like you landed on the moon and stuck your fucking flag in the ground. You think you can just move in here and start staking your flag everywhere?"

"I'm not *claiming* your stupid cat. I collared him as a favor to you. He was wandering around without one, and I didn't want someone thinking he's a stray."

"Everyone out here knows Bodhi, so no one would mistake him for a stray except you. *And* you didn't just tag him, you fucking renamed him. BS? You renamed my cat BS?"

"I didn't—"

"Look, lady, this is my fucking cat, okay? Don't go collaring him. Don't go renaming him. Just leave him be."

There's a spark in her eyes, like I've poured gasoline on her, lit a match, and flicked it—ignition. She erupts.

"Leave him be? How about you and your porch-pissing home invader leave *me* be? Take *your* fucking cat and your shitty attitude and get the fuck off *my* property."

"Gladly." I reach for the snap release on the collar, and it falls off Bodhi's neck, landing unceremoniously with a clatter and jingle. Marching down the steps of her porch and across the yard to the road, I hold my head high like I've won some great battle. But the sinking feeling in my gut tells me I'm the loser here.

∼

Grab a copy of **Hearts on Fire** to keep reading the story of Drew, Chloe, and the cats.

∼

And check out *Hearts to Mend*, the next book in the Hearts of Texas series.

Rico Rodriguez was my first friend, first kiss, and first love. Then he was my first heartbreak.

Seven years ago, he left me and this small town to join the Army. Now he's back, a single dad in search of a second chance.

But I'm not the girl he left behind, and I have no interest in taking a walk down memory lane.

It will take more than his sexy smile, sweet son, and meddling mom to mend this broken heart.

*Hearts to Mend is a sexy, full-length, small town, second chance romance with an own-voices depiction of surviving a major medical crisis. Featuring a single dad hero and a firefighter heroine, Hearts to Mend is Book Two of the Hearts of Texas series, but it can be read as a standalone. Though you really should read Book One (Hearts on Fire), too, because it's fabulous!*

## Lost in Austin Series

PREVIEW

If you're interested in something a little less romcom, a little more gritty, check out my award-winning Lost in Austin series, starting with *Up for Air*.

## CHAPTER 1 - WEDNESDAY, OCTOBER 13, 2004

Am I happy? How would I know? What is the measure of happiness?

Up until yesterday, the last day of my twenty-eighth year, I'd naively thought I was happy, or at least not *unhappy*. Like happiness were binary, a light switch you flip on or off—light, dark; happy, sad. Or like one of those creepy clowns who moves his hand across his face as he shifts his expression from one extreme to the other—psycho smile, freaky frown. As if anything in the human condition could be so simple.

Well, there's death, I guess. Death *is* pretty simple. You can't get much more binary than that—1, 0; alive, dead.

Regardless of what I used to think, my reality is now forever changed, a birthday present I can't return. Here I sit, on the dawn of my twenty-ninth year, at the end of the front row of pews in this quaint little church in this quaint little town, tears streaming down my cheeks, wondering how to quantify my happiness—or rather my unhappiness. It's making me miserable, this little epiphany of mine.

No, *little* is the wrong word. There is nothing little about my revelation. This isn't an idea illuminated by a single incandescent bulb flickering over my head. This dawning irradiates with the flash burn of a nuclear bomb.

I look up, half expecting to see a mushroom cloud filling the chapel with the pulverized debris of my former notions. But there's nothing there, only a clear view of the honey-toned oak beams that hold up the roof and the vaulted tops of the massive stained-glass windows, which flank the parishioners with cheery, colorful mosaics forming various tableaus—Jesus, a lamb, a dove, a star.

At my side, Greg glances up, too, as if to catch a glimpse of whatever it is that's captured my attention. When he sees nothing special, he returns his attention to the pastor at the front of the church.

I sniffle again and blow my nose into the handkerchief Greg's father gave me at the beginning of the service. The wet, snotty sound echoes up to the steeple and bounces against the towering windows, nearly drowning out the voice of Pastor Rick.

I glance at the pastor and catch a glimpse of Grandpa Chuck behind him, his face just visible above the edge of the casket. Speaking of death and its binary morbidity—there lies the reason we are all here today. Charles Elton Hendricks III is dead.

I quickly look away, down at the handkerchief fisted tightly in my lap, smears of black where my mascara has marred the white linen. I can't bear to see him like that. He looks so strange. The mortician has done a good job putting a bit of color in his cheeks to make him look almost alive, just resting. But with his hair combed over and dressed in a light blue suit, he looks like someone else. He looks like the "used car salesman" version of himself.

Grandpa Chuck was a rough and rugged old man whose entire wardrobe consisted of denim overalls and white T-shirts. He had a half-naked woman tattooed on his arm, and if you asked him to, he would make her wiggle while he sang an Elvis tune. He was missing the tips of two fingers on his left hand but could still play a mean guitar; he even played with Bill Monroe a few times. He was a moonshiner back in his youth, a train-hopping hobo for a time, and he spent more than a few nights in jail. He had lived a full, long life—a life of bluster, moxie, and gusto, a life filled with all the best stories. Grandpa Chuck was no used car salesman.

Of all Grandpa Chuck's stories, my favorites were the ones about Millie. His eyes would sparkle, and his smile would stretch wide across his wrinkled face as he'd reminisce about the night he first laid eyes on her.

There was never any doubt in his mind; Millie was his love, his one and only for the seventy-one years they spent together. She took a little convincing, but soon she was just as smitten, and their love never wavered. They were still in love three days ago, when Millie sat beside Grandpa Chuck's hospice bed, squeezing his frail fingers and promising she would see him again soon.

With that thought, tears start to well in my eyes...again. Shit. I'm crying...again.

*Sniff.*

At my left, Greg squeezes my hand and leans close to whisper in my ear. His tone is soothing yet vexed as he asks if I'm okay. It's a dumb question. Do I look okay? I nearly laugh. Jesus, who could laugh at a time like this?

Funny, asking Jesus dumb, rhetorical questions while sitting in a church. That thought almost makes me giggle even more. I cover my mouth with my fist, swallowing the impulse.

Wanting to quell Greg's concern, I try to cry more demurely, but it's impossible. I'm an ugly crier, always have been. Bawling over skinned knees and playground bullies always caused my face to puff up and my cheeks to stain with blotches of bright red, like a half-ripened tomato. It's never been a pretty sight. Without a mirror to check, I can only imagine what I look like right now in my neatly pressed black dress, my long dark hair twisted into a knot at the nape of my neck, my makeup tidy and understated, except for the raccoon bandit mask of smeared mascara and drippy, bloodshot eyes.

The congregation is singing now, "Amazing Grace," but I can't find my voice. I stare down at the pages of the hymnal Greg holds on his lap, my vision swimming in tears. I sniff again and blow my nose, then look up at my husband.

Greg isn't singing either. Sitting with his head lowered, he stares blankly at the song book's tablature. He's as handsome as ever, his classic-Hollywood looks complimented by the smooth lines of his gray suit, his jaw cleanly shaven and his honey-brown hair combed back. But his eyes, normally a warm whiskey color, look steel gray today.

He suppresses a yawn with the back of his hand, and I exhale with relief. That's all it is, exhaustion. Of course he's exhausted. When he received the call about his grandfather's stroke, we'd made the trip from Austin to this corner of Appalachia in one night. We'd wanted a chance to say our goodbyes before Grandpa Chuck passed away three days later. The last week has taken a toll on us all, emotionally and physically.

I reach for Greg's hand and squeeze. He gives me a toothless smile before returning his attention to the song book.

I glance past him to Jake, our best friend, who looks even more dark and intimidating than usual, decked out in all black, his posture ramrod straight, his hands clasped tightly in his lap, and his long jet-black hair plaited into two tight braids that hang down his chest. He sings the hymn lyrics from memory, and despite his imposing physical presence and perpetual scowl, his powerful baritone voice is a welcome, soothing comfort. I listen for a moment before looking back down at the hymnal in Greg's lap, only now noticing it's open to the wrong song.

∽

Outside, Greg, Jake, Greg's brother Matt, and a myriad of Hendricks cousins carry the cherry coffin to a spot beneath the wide branches of a hickory tree. The hole is already dug, and at the head of it sits a wide granite tombstone emblazoned with Hendricks on the back. On the front, Grandma and Grandpa Hendricks's names and birthdates are already etched into the stone. Soon, Grandpa Chuck's death date will be added beside a void beneath Grandma Millie's information, a placeholder marking the time until she joins her husband in eternal slumber.

The morbid inevitability of it sends a cold shiver through me. I look away, distracting myself with the details of the blue pop-up tent set off to the side, three rows of plastic chairs placed for family to sit. But no one is sitting except for Millie. Everyone else seems more interested in stretching their legs as they get in a smoke before the start of the graveside service.

In her black wool dress and wide-brimmed hat, Millie looks tiny, so frail and delicate. For a moment I think how odd it looks to see her sitting alone. If Grandpa Chuck were here, he would have his lanky arm draped over her shoulders, comforting her sorrow away. Then again, if Grandpa Chuck *were* here, she would feel no sorrow.

I can't stand the thought of her alone, so I join her. Leaving Greg and Jake behind, I make my way up the aisle along the edge of the tent and sit beside her. Millie glances at me, then we both stare at the cherry casket surrounded by sprays of fall floral arrangements.

After a moment, Millie quietly laments, "This morning, I read an article in the newspaper that he would have found interesting. I wanted to tell him about it, and then I remembered he's not with me anymore." She pauses. "I miss him."

Fresh tears prick my eyes, and I reach over to squeeze Millie's hand in mine. It's such a small gesture given the wound she's exposed to me, but she places her other palm over my fingers and squeezes in kind. I glance at her, and she smiles at me.

"Ari, it's your birthday today, isn't it?" Millie asks.

I nod, almost embarrassed to admit it.

"How old are you now?"

"I'm twenty-nine."

"Well, goodness. So young and with so much time ahead of you." She leans in, as if to tell me a great secret. "Don't waste a moment of it, honey. It moves so fast, faster than you realize. Cherish the time you have and the people you love."

I force a grin for Millie's sake and try to swallow the lump in my throat. It takes everything in me not to start bawling again. I glance up at Greg, the man I've spent twelve years of my life with, and I try to imagine the next sixty.

I furrow my brow with concentration as Greg glances my way. He returns my anxious expression, then looks past me, just over my shoulder. I watch him a moment longer before I, too, look past my husband to the valley beyond.

Fall leaves fill the landscape with fiery shades of orange, yellow, and red. Despite the cold of the day, the surrounding mountains are ablaze with ardent color, like an inferno stretching down the hillsides to the valley below, ready to engulf us all in flames.

I shiver.

~

In my old bathrobe, I curl up on the bed to look out the window. As I lazily stare, my eyes drift out of focus until the moving shapes of clouds and wavering colors of leaves blur into an abstraction.

Vaguely, I note the sound of the front door closing with a heavy bang. Greg's voice echoes as he calls to me and my parents. He's greeted with only silence. I clear my throat as if to answer, but there's no need.

Greg comes to find me in my old room. Closing the door behind him, he sits on the edge of the bed and stares down at his shoes for a long moment, alone with his thoughts.

The silence between us is unnerving; I speak just to fill the space. "My parents went to take a casserole to your grandma."

Greg nods but doesn't speak, doesn't even look at me. I reach my hand over and lay it on his thigh.

"Greg, I'm sorry about your grandpa. And I'm sorry I was so weepy. I'm not sure what came over me."

Greg shrugs, still staring down at the plush carpet at his feet. I watch him, urging him with a silent plea: *say something, say anything; please, just look at me.*

The telepathy works. Greg turns and looks down at me. His face is blank, the lines rigid and cold, like marble—a beautiful statue. With a tilt of his body, he leans closer to me, bracing his weight on one hand while he uses the other to play with a tendril of my hair, then tucks it behind my ear.

Slowly he leans down and kisses me. It's gentle at first, a delicate brush of his lips over mine, but soon his movements become harder, more urgent and insistent. He twists around until he's stretched out beside me and then on top of me, his weight pressing me deep into the springy, old mattress. I grunt as the air whooshes out of my lungs.

He moves fast, tugging at my robe belt to try to free me from it, but his maneuvers only tighten the terry cloth rope. He settles for pushing the front flaps aside and fixes his mouth to one of my breasts.

"What if my parents come home?" I can't remember the last time we had sex in my old bedroom. Probably before we were married. The idea excites me almost as much as it excited me the first time—on the night of my eighteenth birthday when I snuck him through my window, and he took my virginity.

"We'll be quiet," he says with a rough edge to his words. "Please, Ari, I need you right now."

At my nod, he fumbles with the zipper on his pants and enters me with a sharp thrust. I gasp at the sudden fullness, wince at the pinch of pain, but soon my body relaxes, excites. I arch my back as I brace one palm against the headboard and use the other to grab at him, my nails pressing sharp through the fabric of his slacks, spurring him on. With each stride, his tempo increases until he's grunting as he moves hard and deep into me. I can't help but come. I'm easy like that. I freeze and spasm and bite his neck to muffle my cries, and my climax triggers his. He lets out a groan, then, spent, collapses on top of me.

Lying beneath my husband on my childhood bed, his weight pressing down on me, I can't help but cry. I'm easy like that too. Greg pushes up onto an elbow, staring down at me in panic, worried he's hurt me in some way. The stricken look on his face saddens me even more. Tears slip from the corners of my eyes as I lean up and gently kiss him. Relieved, he drops to my side and gathers me in his arms, hugging me close to his chest.

Whatever dam existed within me washes away, and I am overcome with tears. I sob uncontrollably, sometimes moaning loudly and other times heaving and shaking with silent convulsions. Greg tenderly strokes my hair and whispers soothing sounds into my ear, patiently letting me cry until I run dry. Then we lie together in silence.

I'm about to drift off to sleep when Greg curses. "It's the thirteenth. I forgot your birthday."

"Your grandpa died; you're excused."

"I didn't even get you flowers."

Trying to lighten the mood, I point to the assortment of funeral floral arrangements covering every inch of my old desk. Millie had insisted I take a few flowers with me, then loaded me up like a pack mule. "I have plenty of flowers."

Greg barks out a half-hearted laugh. "Well, I'm still sorry."

I give him a toothless grin before I close my eyes, lay my cheek on his chest, and drift off to sleep, finally drawing this birth and death day to a close.

## CHAPTER 2 - SATURDAY, NOVEMBER 13, 2004

I have never been a sad person. But have I ever truly been a happy person? If I am a happy person, wouldn't I know? But how do you know something like that? What are the signs, the symptoms of happiness?

These are the cold, cruel thoughts that ricochet through my head, leaving Swiss cheese holes and torn bits of gray matter in their wake. This is the fallout from my little epiphany bomb, dropped that sad day as I stared at the lifeless face of Greg's grandfather.

On the dawn of my twenty-ninth year, my eyes were opened to the revelation of my own eventual demise, my finite mortality reflected back at me from the grave. And those thoughts were not buried alongside Charles Elton Hendricks III. They infected me; they infect me still—growing, feeding, eating away at me like a necrotic wound.

Frustratingly, the thoughts that ping and pierce my mind like little bits of shrapnel are neither helpful nor actionable. They come at me in the form of useless bumper sticker sentiments like:

"Life is short. Live it."

"Are you Carpeing your Diem?"

"Don't worry, be happy."

But I am happy, aren't I? I mean, I'm pretty sure I'm not *unhappy*. Doesn't that count for something?

I shake my head as I turn the corner and walk farther into the neighborhood of midcentury ranch-style homes. On my left, I spot the remains of some poor, dead creature flattened in the middle of the road. I hold my breath, not wanting to breathe in the carrion scent that calls to the buzzards circling above. Thankful I have my dreary thoughts to distract me from the morbid tableau, I quicken my pace until I'm far enough away not to smell the rot when I take a deep breath of the fresh air.

If happiness is not binary, not black and white but rather a spectrum of gray, then what shade of gray am I? Am I charcoal, gunmetal, slate? Maybe my happiness is taupe. Is taupe even a shade of gray, or is it more of a beige? Hell, maybe my shade of happiness is beige. *For fuck's sake, please don't let my happiness be* beige.

If I could choose, I'd opt for a heather-gray sort of happiness, flecks of light and dark blending together to form my own personal shade of middle of the road. But what is that emotion, the one in the middle? When you're neither overwhelmed with joy nor drowning in sorrow, do you simply wallow in some muddy shade of numbness?

Talk about wallowing. I roll my eyes at my whiny inner monologue as I cross a footbridge over the creek and move deeper into the small city park nestled within the urban neighborhood.

Clearly, I'm in a funk. This is nothing new. It always happens when Greg goes away on business. I suck at being alone. It's a character flaw. Alone, I tend to retreat into my head, and that's only ever a good thing when I'm writing. This time, though, is worse than usual. Just one week into Greg's two-week stint in Singapore, and I'm already going on daily hours-long walks so I don't suffocate as the walls close in on me.

I hug my jacket closed as I approach a bench near the edge of the water. It's Beatrice and Samuel Dickson's bench, dedicated in 2001, or so the little brass plaque screwed to the green metal slats reads. Settling onto Bea and Sam's bench, I let the quiet babble of the brook soothe my addled mind.

After a moment's repose, I pull my notebook out of my satchel, click my pen into action, and hover the tip over the page. Nothing comes. The black ballpoint leaves little tick marks on the paper, but no words make their way there. After too long waiting for inspiration to strike, I give up and stuff it all back into my bag, then hug my knees to my chest as I take in the scenery.

It's too late in the year for most of the birds, but the crisp breeze blowing through the naked branches of the trees is enough white noise to distract me from my dreary state of mind. And down on the leaf-strewn ground, a ginger-toned squirrel busies himself with the task of finding and burying pecans for foraging later in the season.

There's a shrill whistle, and the squirrel scurries up a tree. I yelp and cover my head as I twist around to identify the source of the sound.

Jake.

Shielding his eyes from the glare of the afternoon sun, he stares up the tree where the squirrel fled. With his long hair down past his shoulders and wearing his old leather jacket over a ratty Megadeth T-shirt, Jake looks much like he did when I first met him over a decade ago. Still tall, dark, and handsome, with a metalhead ensemble that makes him look mid-twenties rather than his actual age of thirty-two.

"Did you see the testicles on that big, brassy son of a bitch?"

"Huh?"

Not waiting for an actual answer, Jake braces his hand on the bench, then swings his legs over the back and flops onto the seat beside me with a harrumph. He stretches his legs and lights a cigarette, offering me a drag, as he always does. I refuse, as I always do.

"That squirrel's balls were *huge*. Like, a third of his overall body weight. Can you imagine if humans lugged around *cajones* like that? It'd be like sporting a pair of watermelon in my Fruit of the Looms."

I blink, and Jake chuckles, succeeding once more at his favorite pastime, the *Stun-Ari-Speechless* game.

"Well," Jake blows a puff of smoke into the wind, "how's it hangin'?"

The sound I make resembles "meh," which earns me a cockeyed scowl from Jake.

"I'm gonna need more words outta you, sis, unless you want me to do all the talking." He pauses to give me a window to speak, which he promptly closes. "Did you know that Brass Balls up the tree there has a bone in his penis? A legit 'boner,' the lucky little fucker." Another brief pause for a puff of smoke. "Actually, most mammals have a *baculum*—that's the Latin name for penis bone. Humans and spider monkeys are the only primates who don't—"

"Are you happy?"

"—have a boner bone."

Jake stares at me—this time he's the one who's stunned speechless—and I stare back at him, waiting for an answer.

"Happy?" He shrugs. "Sure."

"How do you know?"

Jake cocks his head to the side to give me a proper scowl. "The fuck are you talking about?"

"How do you know you're happy? It's a simple question." I hug my legs tighter to my chest and rest my chin on my knees, watching him as he considers his answer.

And consider it, he does, furrowing his brow as he takes a long drag on his cigarette. After a moment, he says, "I don't know. I mean, I've got great friends, a pretty decent band, I can pay my rent each month, I've got my health..." After a long exhale, he cocks an eyebrow and adds, "Plus, I'm ridiculously good looking, practically drowning in eager pussy, and I've got a girlfriend who can suck the chrome off a trailer hitch. Happy doesn't begin to cover it, darlin'. I'm fuckin' ecstatic."

I roll my eyes. "Deep thoughts with Jake Sixkiller. I should have known better."

Jake extinguishes his smoke on the sole of his boot and turns to face me, assuming the thoughtful pose of a therapist on the clock. "What's brought all this up, little sis?"

I stutter and stammer as I try to explain. "I don't think I'm very happy. But I don't think I'm unhappy either. I think I'm...neither...which is what scares me. It's like I'm just sort of existing without feeling, like I'm numb. Which seems like utter bullshit, right? I mean, I listen to your list, and I nod and I say to myself, 'Yep, yep, uh huh, me too.' I have a great family. I have Greg. I have you. I have a roof over my head, and I don't have to work some shit job to pay for it. I have my health. I have…plenty. So why am I not, you know, more… happy?"

"Maybe it's PMS? You know, sometimes you get a tad emotional, and—"

"One more word, and I swear I'll punch you in your goddamn squirrel sac, Jacob Mitchell Sixkiller. I mean it."

Jake smirks.

"I think I'm going through a midlife crisis."

"Twenty-nine is only midlife if you plan to die by sixty, little sis. Don't get ahead of yourself."

"Semantics. My point is, I'm going through a…thing. I've been taking stock, and while I have all these things in my life that should make me happy, all I seem to focus on are the things that are missing."

Jake goes bug-eyed, and his posture snaps ramrod straight as he gawks at me. "Holy fucking shit, Ari. Are you talking about babies? Is *that* what this is about?"

I shake my head decisively. No, this is not about babies. In fact, in the month since the funeral, as I've assessed my wants and needs, the thought of having a child didn't even occur to me. I've never once felt the tick of my biological clock. And I'm fairly certain a child is not the thing missing in my life. But it's telling this was the first conclusion Jake jumped to. At twenty-nine, I'm supposed to want kids, aren't I? That's the norm, that's the life path most taken, but here I go through the bramble and bushes off to the far left, wanting not babies, but—

"Then what is it that's missing? What are we talking about here?" Jake asks.

In that moment, I want to tell him everything. I look into his warm eyes, and I see my best friend and closest confidant, the person I've shared everything with over the last decade. I want to stare him straight in the eyes, not flinching or stammering as I open my mouth and speak the truth of what I'm feeling: *I want to live. I want to breathe free. I want to explore my limits and try new things. I want to see and taste and smell and touch the world around me.* I catch my breath, the excitement bubbling through me even though I'm only saying these words in my head. With new air in my lungs, I raise my imaginary voice even louder as I boldly declare: *I want to fuck and suck and scream and come. I want to travel the world and dance naked in the rain and howl at the moon. I want to love and lust and laugh. I want to hurt and scorn and cry. I want to feel…everything.*

Shit, I'm going to cry again. I look down at my boots and tug at the laces, tying them into double knots.

Jake clasps my fists in his. "What's going on? What aren't you saying?"

I panic. What can I say? I can't tell him any of this. Every time I open my mouth to speak the truth, I see a flash of images: Greg's face on the day we met, his smile on the day we married, the look he gives me when he makes love to me, the way he kisses me before he leaves for his long trips.

Everything I'm feeling now is a betrayal of him. Doesn't the mere fact I want more than what I have suggest what I have is insufficient, that Greg is not enough? I snap my lips shut like a child about to cross her heart and throw away the key that will unlock all her secrets. There is no way I can voice any of these thoughts or desires. In fact, I've already said too much. Jake isn't just my best friend, he's Greg's as well. The two of them have been practically inseparable since they were fourteen years old. What sort of nonsense was I thinking when I called Jake and asked him to meet me, explaining that I needed to talk? I can't talk to him about any of this.

"Ari Beth, babe, talk to me."

I can't bear the look in his eyes, such concern, so I open my mouth, stammering vaguely, "I don't know. I guess I just want…new experiences."

"Experiences?"

"Yeah." I want to end it there, but I know there is no way Jake will leave this alone. So I expound with ambiguity. "Don't you ever feel like you've missed out? Like you took a wrong turn somewhere and now you're miles away from where you want to be, and you've had your face stuck in a map the whole time, so you haven't even been watching the scenery as you've gone by."

Jake reaches his hand up to feel my forehead for a fever.

I chuckle at the gesture. "I sound crazy, don't I?"

Jake holds up his fingers a pinch apart to illustrate that *yes, I do sound a little bit crazy.* But, back on topic, he gives me a shrug and admits, "I'm sorry, little sis, but I don't know what you're talking about."

Of course he doesn't. I'm talking to a man who has never declined anything. Jake is a marvel to me, always has been. Fearing nothing, he will try anything at least once. We are opposites in that way—him guided by curiosity and a live-fast-die-young approach to life and me ruled by fear. Since the death of his family when he was a kid, Jake's thrown caution to the wind, living life in the moment, fully aware it could end at any time.

I'm vaguely aware of the same thing, so why am I so reserved? Throw caution to the wind? What a joke. I wrap myself in caution, like it's a fuzzy blanket on a cold night. All my life, I've taken the safe road, the path of least resistance. And where has it gotten me? Chafed and smothered by the boundaries of my small little life.

I scratch my too tight skin until Jake grabs my hands to stop me. "Are you okay, Two Shoes?"

*Two Shoes.* Jake's nickname for me. It sounds like an Indian name, but actually it's a reference to an Adam Ant song—"Goody Two Shoes" —he used to sing to me.

It took exactly one week working at my first job at the bookstore in the mall—Jake the pothead assistant manager and me the hardworking high schooler—for my name to transform from Ariana "Ari" Goody to Goody Two Shoes to just plain Two Shoes. The nickname stuck. Two Shoes is the name Greg knew me by when we first met. There are people in the various bands that Jake has performed with over the years who only ever knew me as Two Shoes. And I didn't mind. It never bothered me. It had always been accurate; I *was* a Goody Two Shoes.

But now, I do mind. Now, it does bother me. I don't want to be a *good* girl anymore. I don't want to live a cautious, safe life just to get to the end and look back with regret at every adventure I didn't take. I want to be more like Jake and Grandpa Chuck, to live a life of bluster, moxie, and gusto.

I clear the lump from my throat. "I'm fine, Jake. I'm just... fine."

Jake's jaw moves like he's chewing on the gristle of my lie and can't quite swallow it. With a shake of his head, Jake turns away from me, and we both watch the squirrels go about their business.

To be here with my friend yet with this silence is a miserable punishment, a prison akin to solitary confinement. I want to cry and scream and confess everything. Instead, I inspect my fingernails.

Jake reaches into his pocket and produces his pack of cigarettes and a lighter. This time, for the first time in as long as I can remember, he doesn't offer me a puff.

This time, I want one. "May I?" I ask, holding my hand out.

Jake looks confused.

I point at his cigarette, when I say, "I want to try it."

"Smoking?"

I nod.

"No."

"What?"

"No."

"But," I huff "you always offer."

"And you always decline."

"Well, this time I'm not declining. Gimme."

"No."

"What the hell, Jake?" My voice ratchets up to a yell, full of righteous indignation. "Some friend you are."

"Is this what you're talking about? Is this the *new experience* you want to try? Nicotine addiction? That's just dumb, Ari."

"If *I'm* dumb for wanting to try *your* cigarette, then what does that make you? I mean, besides a giant asshole."

Jake smirks at me, but his breath hisses out of him like steam escaping a kettle. "I'm sorry. You're not dumb."

The last of my steam seeps out as well. "I'm sorry too. You're not a giant asshole, just medium-sized."

Jake tries to hide his grin as he extends the cigarette toward me. I squeal like a kid on Christmas as I awkwardly accept the small gift. Before he's even halfway through his instructions for how I'm supposed to work the thing, I stick the filter end between my lips and suck in a deep breath. Then I nearly cough up a lung…and breakfast…and last night's dinner. When I can finally breathe without dry heaving, I hear Jake chuckling at my side and raise my watery eyes to scowl at him.

"How's that new experience treatin' ya, Two Shoes?"

～

I catch the phone on the fourth ring and pinch the receiver between my cheek and shoulder as I breathlessly answer.

"Everything okay? Sounds like you wrestled the phone from the jaws of a tiger." Greg's voice sounds distant, but ten thousand miles of separation will do that to a voice.

"Yeah, Austin's changed a lot since you left last week. Tigers everywhere."

That earns me a laugh from the other end of the world.

"How's Singapore?" I make my way back to the kitchen, scrubbing the sauce pan I'd used to make dinner.

"I haven't had much time to explore, but so far my impression is it's big and crowded. You'd hate it."

"Why do you say that? You never know—I might love it."

Greg scoffs, clearly skeptical, but wisely changes the subject. "So what are you doing, and more importantly, what are you wearing?"

In my sexiest voice, I inform him, "I'm in the kitchen, bent over the sink. I'm wet…dripping, wearing your Slayer T-shirt."

That earns me a low groan. "Which one?"

"South of Heaven, and I'm not wearing any underwear." That part's not true. I'm actually wearing my most comfortable granny panties in addition to a pair of his old sweatpants rolled up three times at the ankles and fluffy winter socks covered in little snowmen.

I can tell he appreciates my editorial decision by the hitch in his breath. "Keep talking. I need to hear your voice."

And so I do. I tell him about my last few days—grocery shopping, trying to write, lunch with Jake, trying to write again, renewing my driver's license, smoking my first cigarette—

"Wait. What?"

"Jake let me have a drag off one of his cigarettes."

"Why?"

"Because I asked."

"Why?"

"Because…I wanted to try it. It's this new thing I'm trying, where I try new things." Feeling an urgency to defend myself, I expound, "I've been thinking…the funeral got me thinking. I mean, you know, we've talked about this before—"

"Ari, he was ninety-two." Math, Greg's pat response. We've had this conversation a couple of times before. It always ends here, with Greg explaining that his grandfather had lived a good, long life and thus my tears were misplaced. What Greg has failed to grasp is my tears are not for Grandpa Chuck.

The thing is—the same math Greg relies on as the basis for his logic is the reason for my turmoil. On that day in October, I'd turned twenty-nine as I stared down at Grandpa Chuck in his cherry box, dead at ninety-two. We were inverse, Grandpa Chuck and me.

It was then, the moment when I'd done the math, my epiphany bomb exploded—a moment of clarity so bright it hurt my eyes, frying my retinas so that nothing would ever look the same again. Grandpa Chuck and me, we were inverse in every way. He'd lived a life filled with epic stories. Me? My life has been small and safe—all soft edges and sanitized surfaces. I have no stories, epic or otherwise.

Drying my hands on a dishrag, I walk the cordless from room to room, pacing as the walls close in. "I'm not talking about Grandpa Chuck. I'm talking about me."

"What do you mean?"

"I mean…life is short. I want to live it." Great, now I'm speaking in bumper-sticker sentiments.

Greg says nothing, and the silence between us is filled with static, a bad connection.

"Greg?"

"Yeah?"

I search for something to say, finally settling on a new subject. "When are you coming home?"

He clears his throat. "I have a meeting with the site engineers today. I'll know more then."

I nod, even though he can't see me.

"It's getting late there. I should let you get some sleep."

"Okay."

"Good night."

"Greg."

"Yeah?"

"I love you."

There's a pause, a hiccup of time between when I say it and when he says it back, but when he speaks there's a smile in his tone. "I love you too. Sweet dreams, sweet thing."

## CHAPTER 3 - SUNDAY, DECEMBER 12, 2004

My eyes have drifted out of focus, but I'm pretty sure I can make out Vincent Van Gogh's self-portrait in the grain pattern of our wood floors. Behind me on the couch, Greg strokes his fingers through my hair as he flips channels on the television. This is our ritual, our together time. When he's not traveling, we easily slip into a regular routine—dinner followed by couch cuddles, his feet on a pillow on the coffee table, my head on a pillow in his lap, his fingers gently stroking my scalp and trailing down my back as we watch old movies.

I remember this being the highlight of my day. The warmth of Greg's lap under my head instilled me with a sense of calm. The tender touch of his fingers twirling strands of my hair sent shivers down my spine. I'd moan at the sensation of his touch, and he'd grin as he'd keep petting me.

When did it stop meaning so much? When did the sweetness, tenderness, and need for constant connection abate? Now, it's just habit. Like a residual haunting, an endless, mindless repeating of a distant memory. It's as if Greg and I aren't here anymore, but our ghosts remain, continuing to pantomime the nuanced details of our daily lives together.

I wince when Greg's fingers reach a particularly stubborn tangle. He tries to be gentle as he works out the knot, but the tugs and pulls send pricks of pain through my scalp and down my spine. I revel in the sensation. I need it. I need to feel *something*. Even if what I'm feeling is pain, it's better than feeling nothing.

"What's with you?" Greg asks as he turns off the television.

My eyes snap into focus. What I thought was Van Gogh's scruffy red beard and long, sharp nose are just knots in the floor's wood grain.

"Talk to me, Ari. It's like you're a million miles away."

I spring up to sit beside him and watch him closely as I ask, "Do you love me, Greg?"

"Yeah, of course."

"Why?"

"What kind of question is that? You're my wife, Ari. Of course I love you."

"Wife—that's a role, not a reason."

Greg grins, like he's laughing at some inside joke. "Come here."

I don't move, still waiting for an answer to my question. He clasps my ankle and gently tugs me onto his lap, my legs straddling his. I let him move me, embrace me. It feels good, being this close to him. I rest my head on his shoulder and breathe in his scent, fresh and clean, soapy.

"Look at me, Ari."

I lift my head.

He tucks a strand of hair behind my ear as he starts rattling off a list: "I love your big brown eyes. I love the little gap between your two front teeth. I love that you dip your pizza in ranch dressing and drown your tacos in salsa." He presses his lips to my neck and gives me a feathery kiss as he takes a deep breath. "I love the way you smell." His tongue darts out and tickles the spot below my ear. "I love the way you taste." Greg pulls away to look me in the eyes again. With one hand, he strokes my temple, then he gives my head a little thump, thump, thump with his thumb. "But mostly I love all the crazy shit you've got going on up here."

I giggle.

"I love your laugh."

I sigh then yelp when he cups my ass in one of his palms.

"I love your ass."

His palm slides so far down my ass that his fingers splay between my thighs and proceed to tease me. I gasp.

"I love that gasp."

Without another word, Greg kisses me. There is no hesitation, no awkwardness. Like a ballet, our kiss is perfect, practiced, a well-choreographed *pas de deux*. After twelve years together, I know his kiss intimately. I know to zig when he zags. I know he starts gentle, the pressure in his lips soft and tender. I know he likes to lick into my mouth with darting little dashes of tongue. Then he palms the back of my head, tangling his fingers in my hair, and groans into my mouth just before the kiss changes, grows deeper. I know to match his increased intensity stroke for stroke, nibble for nibble as our maneuvers grow more ardent and fervid.

We are proficient lovers of one another. Normally, there is a comfort in that. But today, the flawless kiss suffocates, the seasoned touch chafes, our studied embrace constricts.

I twist away from his mouth as I grab two fistfuls of his hair. It feels soft in my hands. I pause for a moment to stroke his head, then yank. Greg's head ratchets back, and I latch onto his neck like a vamp. Starting just above his collarbone, I bite, suck, and lick my way up to his jaw.

Nothing about the way I kiss Greg is studied or choreographed. I attack him, feral and ferocious, a cat pouncing on her prey. My teeth gnash against his as we each fight for control. His hands fist my hair, too, and he's locked with me in a power struggle as we challenge one another with bites and licks, nibbles and tastes.

I feel Greg's excitement rigid against my thigh. He pulls his hands from the tangle of my hair and slides them down my back to cup and squeeze my ass with bruising force.

I whisper a command, "Take me to bed."

His response rumbles in his chest. "No. I'm taking you right here."

We're like a couple of teenagers, all arms and elbows as we strip each other in a frenzy. There's a tear of fabric when Greg pulls my shirt over my head. I paw at his jeans, and he tugs at my bra, a tangle of fumbling fingers working to spring clasps, pop buttons, and yank zippers.

When we're finally both naked, Greg gets me flat on my back and hovers above in a stiff plank, not kissing me, not touching me, just watching. He's always liked the look of anticipation that dawns over my face right before he fucks me. He savors it now, a smug grin on his lips as I wiggle beneath him, my frustration an itch I need him to scratch. I open my legs wide, twisting them up on his back, as if to climb and mount him from below.

Catching me by surprise, he suddenly lets his weight fall. Greg is a lean man, tight with muscle, but not overly large, yet still he crushes me beneath him, forcing the air out of my lungs. Before I recover my breath, he spears into me, burying himself to the hilt.

The feeling sends a burst of energy through every synapse in my body, lighting me up like a Vegas sign. I love that about sex; it has the singular power to give me everything I need, right when I need it. Like being zapped with a pair of defibrillator paddles, I'm jolted out of arrest. My senses come alive with stunning acuity, suddenly able to taste and feel and hear and smell and touch *everything*.

I arch my back as he moves faster and deeper inside me. I curl my limbs around him, pressing up to meet his hips with each stroke. I come, hard, and holler up at him, holding his gaze when I'm able to keep my eyes open.

Greg loves to watch me come, and when I do, it usually brings him with me. It does now too. His eyes grow large as he presses deep and freezes, groaning with ecstasy before he collapses, spent.

We lie naked, wrapped in a knot of legs and arms, our faces cocooned in a tangle of my hair. He shifts to the side and gently arranges me above him so he's no longer crushing me. I rest my head on his chest and sigh at the sensation of his fingers tracing the curve of my lower back.

"Jesus Christ." Greg exhales a loud gust of breath. In a drowsy, sex-laden whisper he asks, "What's gotten into you? I think you've left marks."

I grin as I look at the hickey on his neck, feeling a strange sense of pride in leaving my brand on him.

"Is that what you meant by trying new things?"

The question surprises me. We haven't broached this subject since our brief conversation during his Singapore trip nearly a month ago. I can't believe he even remembers. Without thinking, I throw out a casual reply. "That...and other stuff."

"Other stuff, eh?" He gets a devilish glint in his eyes as he smooths his hand down my backside and gooses me. Of course, the final frontier *would* be Greg's first thought. He's asked to be my back-door man more than once. My answer has always been a firm no.

I squeal and squirm in his arms. "That hadn't made my list."

Greg chuckles and slides his hand back up to safe territory. I relax again. But as I start to think about it, I open my mind to the possibility. Why not say yes next time? The only thing to fear is fear itself, right? Well, there's the fear of pain, but it can't hurt *that* much, can it? Nothing ventured, nothing gained, and venturing into butt stuff would surely be a big leap—a bootylicious bounce if you will—toward living a life of bluster, moxie, and gusto.

"There's a list?" Greg asks with a yawn. "What's on it?"

There isn't actually a list in the strictest sense of the word; nothing has been committed to paper yet. It's more like a Möbius strip of thoughts, ideas, and fantasies that has floated around in the back corners of my mind. But a few ideas do continue to surface. "I want to get drunk. I'm twenty-nine, and I've never been drunk. That's kind of pathetic. So, yeah, I want to get drunk."

"Mm-hmm," he mumbles drowsily.

"Also, I'd like to kiss a girl."

Greg's eyes rocket open. "What?"

I don't repeat myself. He heard me.

"Any specific girl in mind?"

I shake my head.

"Well, when you find this mystery girl you want to kiss, can I watch?"

I'm stunned by his nonchalant response. I've told him I want to kiss another person, and he thinks it's hot? Then again, we are talking about a woman, and men so rarely feel threatened by women.

"What if I were to say that I wanted to kiss another guy?"

Greg's fingers stiffen on my hips, and his eyes narrow as he asks, "Any specific guy in mind?"

I shake my head.

"Why do you want to kiss another guy?"

"I didn't say that I want to kiss another guy. I just asked what you would say if I did."

"What are we talking about here, Ari?" Greg squints at me like he's trying to see through skin and bone and catch a glimpse of what's in my head.

Not sure how to answer him, I ask, "In all your travels, have you ever met a woman who you wanted to be with?"

"Are you asking me if I've ever cheated on you? Because I've never done that, Ari Beth."

"But surely you've been attracted to other women, right? You've thought about it?"

"There is a big difference between thinking about something and doing it." He answers without answering.

"What if we were to agree it's okay to act on those desires?"

"Are we really having this conversation?" Greg shifts beneath me, gently detangling our limbs, then sits upright. "Because if we are, I, uh, I need a beer."

I nod.

With a fortifying breath, like he's about to dive underwater, Greg slides his boxers back on and walks into the kitchen.

I remain unmoved, alone and naked on the couch, staring up at the stilled ceiling fan overhead. Feeling too exposed, I jolt upright and search for my clothes. They're strewn about the room, my jeans inside out in a pile on the floor. I wrestle the denim to extricate my underwear, then hurriedly pull them on. They're inside out, too, but I don't care. I need cover for this conversation; any cover will do.

Greg hollers, "You want a beer?"

The words *no, thanks* balance on the tip of my tongue, but when I open my mouth to answer, I surprise myself by saying, "Yes, please."

Greg returns with two bottles of beer, handing me one as he settles onto the far cushion of the couch, a gulf of leather between us. When he extends his beer toward me, I hesitate before clinking my bottle against his, surprised by the casual toast. He takes a sip, and so do I. Curling my nose at the strange flavor, I set mine aside.

After another drink, Greg asks, "What's this all about?"

I take a deep breath, and before I can stop myself, I blurt it out, saying the words that once said cannot be unsaid, words that once voiced could change everything: "I want to open our marriage."

Greg considers, then, finally, he speaks. "Why?"

I begin to panic, babbling as my only defense. "It was the funeral that got me thinking about all the amazing things your grandpa had done in his life, all the crazy stories. By contrast, I realized how small my life is." I backpedal when

Greg flinches. "I don't mean *small*. I just mean..." I huff, frustrated that I can't express myself coherently. I'd read an article about polyamory last month, and it set my imagination loose. Now I see I should have done more research, learned the lexicon, because right now, when I need them most, the right words escape me. "I'm not putting any of this on you. My life isn't small because of you...I mean my life isn't *small*, it's... limited."

Greg says nothing.

So I talk more. "I love you, Greg. I've loved you since I was seventeen, and that hasn't changed. But sometimes I feel like we've limited ourselves by committing to each other so young. Or maybe it's just me; I've closed myself off to the world outside."

Pausing, I swallow hard, but I can't get the lump out of my throat. I pull my feet up onto the couch, and Greg does the same. We sit with our legs against our chests, as if our knees are armor and can provide an adequate defense for our hearts.

"I think I just want the space...the freedom to experience the world around me, on my terms, and I want to give you that freedom too."

"And you think opening our marriage will give you the freedom you need?"

"Us. It will give *us* that freedom. And yes, I think it will."

"Why can't you experience the world with me, with *just* me?"

My spirits sink. My fortitude collapses like a house of cards. "Yeah, you're right." I rest my cheek on my knees. "I've been in a weird mood lately. Forget I said anything."

"No." Greg sets his beer aside and brushes his fingers across my feet to get my attention. "Ari, I'm not arguing with you. I'm trying to understand where this is coming from. Because let's be clear: What you're asking for is permission to fuck other guys, right? That's the bottom line." Greg's tone isn't angry or harsh in any way. Even as he says the word *fuck,* he enunciates clearly, his tone phlegmatic. It's like we're entering a debate, and he's formulated his rebuttal.

I try to read him, to get some sense of where his emotions lie. And that's when he surprises me with the hint of a smile. It's exactly what I need to regain my courage and continue this. I take a deep breath, and he does too. I steel my spine, and he adjusts as well. I stare straight at him as he levels those warm, whiskey-colored eyes at me. And I speak, finally sharing the thoughts I've stewed over for months.

"I'm almost thirty, and I feel like I've done so little. I skipped all the normal parts of being twenty-something. I've never been drunk, never been to a raging party, never had a one-night stand or a threesome, never gotten high… I've created this comfortable bubble and existed within it for as long as I can remember. And in the meantime, all these parts of life have passed me by. I just want the chance to experience them, to experience all parts of life."

"Ari, for someone in their twenties, you've done a lot with your life. You know that, right? You're a published author, for Christ's sake. That's not nothing."

I don't know what to say, so I shrug and then hate myself for shrugging. What a lazy expression a shrug is, and this is no time for lazy expressions.

"Okay." Greg chews the inside of his lip, deep in thought. "Let's say we agree to this, hypothetically. Would there be any ground rules?"

Ground rules? Holy shit, are we really talking about this? "Of course there would be ground rules," I say before I've thought it through.

"Like what?"

I have no idea. "What do you have in mind?"

He hardly takes any time to think before he blurts out, "Not Jake."

Jake, as in my best friend who I consider a brother?

"I can't deal with you being with him. Also, we need to promise each other that any extra-marital activity will be safe. I know you're on the pill, but outside of us, it's different. We should always use condoms when we're with anyone else."

I'm stunned. I don't know where I thought this conversation would go, but I wasn't expecting it to go here. Though it does seem fitting Greg would gloss over my ethereal ideas of freedom and space and focus entirely on practical matters like rubbers and safety. After all, Greg is an engineer, a scientist who approaches all aspects of his life with the objective detachment of an observer. To him, this open-marriage thing is just a chemistry experiment—add part A to part B, get a reaction.

I finally squawk out a hoarse, "Okay."

"Do you have any ground rules for me?"

"I...I don't know. Can I think about it?"

Greg shrugs. *No shrugging,* maybe that should be a ground rule. After a moment, he speaks, and I'm not exactly sure what he means when he says, "Okay."

"Okay?"

"We can open the marriage. But if it starts to cause problems between us, we close it. You and me, Ari, that's what's important."

I never imagined we'd get this far in the conversation, so I'd never given any of this serious thought. The longevity of our open marriage was not something I had even considered. How could I not have thought it through before bringing it up?

Jesus, I'm such a child. I'm a little girl playing dress up in a woman's body. I've managed to get older without ever actually growing up. And now, here I am, negotiating the terms of an open marriage with my husband as if I have the slightest notion what I'm talking about. But I guess I better grow up fast because apparently this is happening.

"Okay," I respond.

"Okay," he repeats.

This is surreal. Should it hurt that he's not jealous or possessive? His detachment is almost an affront, and it takes me a moment to remember: this was my goddamn idea.

"Okay," I say again.

Greg reaches for me, stroking the top of my foot with the back of his fingers. I link my pinkie with his, and we sit like this for a moment, quiet, thoughtful, connected.

Then, completely in sync, we dive at each other and tangle together, a twisting mass of lips and limbs. As we kiss and touch and explore each other anew, I feel a growing and nearly overwhelming rush of nervous energy. It's euphoric, this promise of freedom. It fizzes and bubbles and explodes through me like uncorked champagne.

I climb on top of Greg as he tugs his boxers out of the way. With the sound of torn fabric, I push my underwear aside, and we both moan when we connect. We move fast and hard, fucking like wild beasts.

I scream when I come. *Oh holy fuck.* More than just uncorked, my bottle of champagne is shattered into a million pieces, as if christening some new sea vessel.

This is going to be a wild ride.

∽

Grab a copy of ***Up for Air*** to keep reading about Ari's journey of self discovery.

And check out the other books of the Lost in Austin series.

Sex and rock & roll are my top priorities. I mean, let's face it, they're my only priorities.

As frontman of Austin's most popular metal band, I have it all. But when a car accident nearly kills my best friend, I'm rocketed back to memories of that horrible night, all those years ago when I lost my family at the hands of a drunk driver.

That's trauma I'd rather leave buried, so when Nicole, aka Arson Nic, the roller derby dynamo, skates into my bed, I'm more than happy to bury myself in her sweet solace. What I don't expect is to wake up with feelings.

When a once-in-a-lifetime tour opportunity takes me back to the Cherokee reservation where I grew up, I'll have to face the past I buried long ago if I want to take the road home to a future with Nicole.

Book two of the award-winning Lost in Austin series, The Road Home, is an interracial rockstar/roller derby romance that can be read as a standalone. It was the 2022 winner of the Readers' Favorite Gold Medal for Romance – Sizzle and a 2022 Next Generation Indie Book Awards Finalist for Multicultural Fiction.

When I agreed to my wife's request for an open marriage, I didn't anticipate she'd fall in love with another man and leave me.

Alone now and drowning in self-destruction, I cling to memories of a trip to New Orleans nine months ago—the night I wandered into a movie theater called Paradise and spent an evening talking with the beautiful owner, Violet Devollier. Our connection was brief but intense.

It was a connection so intense that when Hurricane Katrina

devastates New Orleans, I'll stop at nothing to return to Paradise and find Violet.

But what good is a broken man in a broken city? To have any chance of a future with Violet, I'll have to find the courage to piece myself back together as we rebuild Paradise after the storm.

Book three of the award-winning Lost in Austin series, After the Storm, is a slow burn interracial romance which can be read as a standalone. It was the 2023 winner of the Readers' Favorite Honorable Mention for Romance – Sizzle.

It's been five years since I found my family. Not my bio-family—my found family of friends. I love them to pieces, but lately they aren't enough.

I want a baby.

All my friends have family units with cuddly babies, and I want that too. But I turn thirty-five in less than a month.

Clock's ticking, so I've got to hustle. I need some baby batter to bake a bun in my oven as soon as possible.

One problem: baby batter comes from men, and I'm really tired of men and their heartbreaker BS.

Manic, though, is different from the other men. A retired sideshow circus performer with piercings all over the place, he's different from everyone. I really like him, and I think he really likes me, too, but he flat out refuses to get me pregnant.

Is Manic worth giving up my dream of being a kickass mom? Maybe.

The fourth and final book of the award winning Lost In Austin series, All the Rest is a grumpy/sunshine romance with tons of laughs and heart and dirty, dirty smut. It's the last book in the series, but it can be read as a standalone.

*Thank you*

Thank you for reading *Wishing Upon a Star*. If you enjoyed the story of Griffin & Scarlet, please spread the word!

xoxo,
Christina

~

And don't forget to subscribe to my newsletter
or join my reader's group for
the latest news and new releases.

subscribepage.io/Td7TPB
facebook.com/groups/christinaswildberries

*Silver Lining Series*

Wishing Upon a Star was originally published as part of the multi-author Silver Lining series. Check out the other books in the series.

∼

Do you believe in magic?

Neither did Shawn until he started bartending at the Silver Lining in Tahoe. The tradition there is to make a wish, write it on a dollar, and pin the dollar to the wall. If the dollar falls, the wish comes true.

Join Shawn as he watches one customer after another's wishes come true and six couples find their silver lining.

1. *Wishing on Snowflakes* by Natalie Parker
2. *Wishing for Always* by LM Dalgleish
3. *Wishing Upon a Star* by Christina Berry
4. *Wishing for More* by Jenni Bara

5. *Wishing to be Yours* by AJ Ranney
6. *Wishing for Champagne Kisses* by Brittanee Nicole

# Acknowledgments

Wishing Upon a Star was originally published as part of the multi-author Silver Lining series. And that series never would have happened if it weren't for Erica Walsh. She started the "Peen Posse" group so a bunch of dirty-minded romance writers could chat about writing and hot dudes. Hence the name.

Working with these wonderful writers (both those in the series, and those who couldn't join the series) has been an absolute pleasure. And having a place to go when I need to laugh or cry or vent about all this indie-author stuff has been a blessing.

As always, huge thanks to my family and my family of friends. I am blessed beyond measure for all the badass people in my life.

To my best friend (aka my husband), who once dyed his hair platinum blonde for Halloween to be my Blondie Bear for a day: I sure do love you.

And of course, a big acknowledgement to James Marsters's for his masterful portrayal of Spike, the inspiration for this Fifty Shades/Twilight-style fan fic romance.

## About the Author

Christina Berry is an award-winning author of sex-positive contemporary romance. Her debut novel, *Up for Air*, won "Sexiest Consent" in the 2021 Good Sex Awards, and her first two Lost in Austin series books won the Readers' Favorite Gold Medal in Romance - Sizzle in 2021 and 2022.

A citizen of the Cherokee Nation, Christina is originally from Oklahoma, and currently resides in Austin, Texas. When not writing, she's usually helping her husband with their never-ending home remodeling adventure or marathon watching true crime television.

WWW.CHRISTINABERRY.COM

facebook.com/christinaberryauthor
instagram.com/authorchristinaberry

Made in United States
Troutdale, OR
05/09/2025